Amanda Minnie Douglas

Kathie's Soldiers

Amanda Minnie Douglas

Kathie's Soldiers

ISBN/EAN: 9783337308018

Printed in Europe, USA, Canada, Australia, Japan

Cover: Foto ©Andreas Hilbeck / pixelio.de

More available books at **www.hansebooks.com**

THE DRAFT. — Page 32.

KATHIE'S STORIES

BY
Miss A. M. Douglas.

ILLUSTRATED

KATHIE'S SOLDIERS.

LEE & SHEPARD, BOSTON.

KATHIE'S SOLDIERS.

BY

AMANDA M. DOUGLAS,

AUTHOR OF " KATHIE'S THREE WISHES," " KATHIE'S AUNT RUTH," " KATHIE'S
SUMMER AT CEDARWOOD," " IN THE RANKS," " KATHIE'S HARVEST
DAYS," " IN TRUST," ETC.

BOSTON:
LEE AND SHEPARD, PUBLISHERS.
1877.

UNIVERSITY PRESS: WELCH, BIGELOW, & CO.,
CAMBRIDGE.

TO

JENNIE M. SUYDAM.

———◆———

"Nor to thyself the task shall be
    Without reward ; for thou shalt learn
    The wisdom early to discern
    True beauty in utility."

WOODSIDE, 1870.

Kathie Stories.

———

CONTENTS.

CHAPTER VIII.

CHAPTER IX.

CHAPTER X.

CHAPTER XI.

CHAPTER XII.

CHAPTER XIII.

CHAPTER XIV.

KATHIE'S SOLDIERS.

CHAPTER I.

ENLISTING IN THE GRAND ARMY.

"HURRAH!" exclaimed Robert Alston, swinging
his hat in the air, as he came up the path; "hurrah! there's going to be a draft at Brookside!
Won't it be jolly?"

The group assembled glanced up at him, — a fair,
fresh, rosy boy, without any cowardly blood in his
veins, as you could easily tell, but given, as such
natures often are, to underrating the silent bravery
of others.

"What will there be so jolly about it, Rob?"
asked his uncle, with a peculiar light in his eye.

"Why, — the whole thing," — and Rob made a
little pause to think, though it did not seem half
so funny now as out on the street with a crowd of
boys, who had been singing at the top of their lungs,
"John Brown's Body," and "My Johnny has gone

for a Soldier," — "the surprise, Uncle Robert, when some of the fellows who have been skulking back and afraid to go find themselves compelled."

"So you think it rather funny to be forced to do what you would not choose of your free-will?" and Uncle Robert gave a queer little smile.

"But —" and Rob looked around considerably perplexed at not finding his argument at hand, and overwhelming. "O, you know what I mean!" throwing himself down upon the grass. "If men have n't patriotism enough to volunteer when their country needs them, why, I think they ought — I just wish I was old enough! I 'd go in a moment. I 'd like the fun of 'marching on'!"

"There is something beside marching," said Kathie, in her soft voice, thinking in a vague way of General Mackenzie.

"Well, I 'd like all of it!"

"The being drafted as well?"

It was Uncle Robert who spoke.

"No, I 'd never be drafted!" and Rob's fair face flushed with a boy's impulsive indignation; "I 'd go at once, — at the first call."

"But if you were a man and had a wife, as well as

bairnies, three or four, or half a dozen, and were compelled to leave them to poverty ? "

" There is the bounty, and the pay."

" Neither of which would be as much as a man could earn in a year at home. And if he never came back — "

" But, Uncle Robert, don't you think it right for a man to be patriotic ? " asked his nephew, in a little amaze.

" Yes. One can never approve of cowardice in any act of life. Still, I fancy there may be a great many brave and good men who have not volunteered, and who, if they are drafted, will do their country loyal service. It may not look quite so heroic, but God, who can see all sides of the question, will judge differently."

" The soldiers don't feel so, Uncle Robert. It seems to me that the men who volunteer *do* deserve a good deal of credit."

" A great many of them do ; but still numbers go for the novelty, or, as you say, the fun. They like a rambling, restless life, and care little for danger, little for death ; but is it an intelligent courage, — the highest and noblest kind ? Does not the man who says, 'If my country in her sorest strait needs me, I will go and do my duty to the utmost,' deserve some credit, especially if he gives up what most men hold most dear ? "

"I believe I did n't look at it in that light altogether. It seemed to me that it was only the cowards and the selfish men who waited to be drafted."

"Then you think I ought to volunteer ? " said Uncle Robert, with a dry but good-natured smile.

There was a very general exclamation.

"You !" exclaimed Rob, aghast at the unlooked-for application.

"I have neither wife nor children. I am young, strong, in good health, and though I do not fancy a military life above all others, I still think I could endure the hardships like a good soldier, and if I stood in the front ranks to face the enemy I do not believe that I should run away."

He rose as he said this, and, folding his arms across his chest, leaned against the vine-covered column of the porch, looking every inch a soldier without the uniform.

It would break his mother's heart to have Uncle

Robert go, and there was Aunt Ruth, and Kathie, and Freddy ; but — what a handsome soldier he would make ! Major Alston, or Colonel Alston, — how grand it would sound ! So you see Rob was quite taken with military glory.

Kathie came and slipped her hand within Uncle Robert's. " We could not spare you," she whispered, softly.

" But if I were drafted ? "

" Well," exclaimed Rob, stubbornly clinging to his point, " the boys over in the village think it will make some fun. There 's a queer little recruiting shanty on the green, and a fifer and a drummer. If our quota is n't filled by next Wednesday, — and they all say it won't be, — the draft is to commence. I 'm glad I 'm not going away until the first of October. I only wish — "

" I wish you were, if that will do you any good," answered Mr. Meredith, glancing up from his book which he had been pretending to read.

" I 'd rather enlist than go to school."

" Maybe enlisting in the home-guard will prove a wise step for the first one."

" Home-guard ? " and Rob looked a bit perplexed.

"Yes. We all do considerable soldiering in our lives unconsciously; and if it comes hard to obey our captains here, I am not sure that we should always find it so easy out on the field. There are some things that take more courage than to march down to the valley of death as did the 'Six Hundred.'"

"O," said Rob, fired again with a boy's enthusiasm, "that's just the grandest thing that ever was written! I don't like poetry as a general thing, it always sounds so girlish to me; but Marco Bozzaris and that are so fine, especially the lines, —

> 'Theirs not to reason why,
> Theirs but to do and die.'

"After all, dying is not the grandest thing," said Aunt Ruth, quietly; "and the detached instances of heroism in one's life have not always required the most courage."

"No, indeed," answered Mr. Meredith, warmly. "I know men who have acquitted themselves bravely under fire, who at home possessed so small an amount of moral courage that they really could not resist temptations which were to their mental and physical detriment."

"But it is the fighting that interests me," said Robert.

"One may be a brave soldier with purely physical courage, but to be a good soldier one needs moral courage as well."

Just then Ada Meredith came down on the porch. She was Kathie's little New York friend, and her uncle had brought her to Cedarwood for a few days. She was growing tall rapidly, and considered herself quite a young lady, especially as she had been to Saratoga with her mother.

So this made a little break in the conversation. Rob somehow did n't get on very well with her; but then he admitted that he did n't like girls anyhow, except Miss Jessie. He was rather glad, therefore, to see Dick Grayson coming up the path, taking it for an excuse to get away.

Ada looked after them with secret mortification. Dick was quite a young man in her estimation, and only that morning he had been very gallant. She hated to have Rob take him off to the lake or any other haunt, so she bethought herself of a little stratagem.

"You promised me a game of croquet," she said to Kathie, with great earnestness.

Kathie glanced up in surprise. When she had proposed it that morning Ada declared it stupid, and said she had grown tired of it. Uncle Robert, knowing nothing of this, answered for her. "Of course," he said; "there are the boys. Rob, don't go away, you are wanted."

Rob made an impatient gesture with his hand, as if he would wave them all out of sight. Uncle Robert walked down to the boys. "Ada would like to play croquet," he remarked, pleasantly.

"I 'm just in the humor for a game myself," answered Dick; but Rob's brow knit itself into a little frown.

"Come, girls!"

Mr. Meredith accompanied them. "We will be umpires," he declared.

Ada chose Dick for a partner. Rob thought it was n't much fun playing with Kathie. He was rather careless, and in the first game they were badly beaten, which made Rob altogether out of humor. Why could n't the girls have stayed on the balcony and talked?

"I can't play!" he said, throwing down his mallet.

Uncle Edward picked it up. "Now, Kathie, let us beat them all to ribbons and fragments!" he exclaimed, gayly, taking her brother's place.

Rob fell out of the ranks to where his uncle stood in the shade of a great tulip-tree.

"Soldiers!" he said, in a low, half-laughing tone.

Rob colored. "I did n't want to play a bit! I wish girls — "

"But a brave soldier goes off of the field after a defeat in good order. If he has done his best, that is all that is required of him."

Rob knew that he had not done his best at all, although he was angry with the mortification of losing the game.

> "Theirs not to reason why,
> Theirs but to do and die,"

said Uncle Robert, using his quotation against him.

"But that does n't mean paltry little matters like this!" — with all a boy's disdain in his voice.

"It means everything when one is right. As Mr. Meredith said a few moments ago, there is a good deal of soldiering in life which must be all voluntary. That ought to suit your ideas. And I think the great Captain is often very patient with us, Rob.

2

He bought us all with a price, you know, whether we serve him or not."

"But it is so hard for me to be"——Rob made a great effort and said, frankly — "good-tempered."

"I do not think that is it altogether."

"What then?" and Rob looked up in a little astonishment.

"We will put it on a military basis, — shirking one's duty because it is not pleasant."

"There was no particular duty about playing croquet!" — in the same surprised tone.

"Why did you do it at all then?"

"Because —"

"Courtesy to a guest becomes a duty in a host."

"But there was Kathie. Dick and I were going down to take a row."

"I have a fancy Dick likes the croqueting as well as he would have liked the rowing."

Dick Grayson's pleasant laugh floated over to them as he said, "Not so bad a beat, after all, Mr. Meredith."

"The life soldiering is not quite so arbitrary. A good deal of it is left to conscience. But if a sentinel at some outpost followed his own devices and let a spy pass the line —"

"He would be shot, of course."

"It seems hard, does n't it, just for one little thing? Yet if one or two men escaped punishment the army would soon be in a state of insubordination. Then when a captain came to lead them in battle each man might consider his way and opinion best. Would it answer?"

"No, it would n't," replied the boy. "But, Uncle Robert, if God had made us — stronger."

"He offers us his strength daily."

"But it is so — I mean you never can think of it at the right moment."

"That is the secret of our duty to him, — to think of his wishes at the right time. He means, in this life, that we shall not seek to please ourselves altogether; but there is no guard-house, no bread-and-water rations, only a still, small voice to remind us."

Rob was silent for some moments, watching the players, and wondering why everything fretted him so easily. Were all the rest of the world to have their own way and pleasures, and he never? "Uncle Robert," he began, presently, "don't you think it fair that I should follow out my own wishes *sometimes?* Is it not unjust to ask me to give up always?'

"Are you asked to give up always?"—and the elder smiled.

"Well—" Rob grew rather red and confused.

"Which would give you the most satisfaction,— to know that you had made two or three people happy, or to enjoy some pleasure alone by yourself? This is the chief thing the Captain asks of us voluntary soldiers; and did not a wise man say that 'he who ruleth his own spirit is greater than he who taketh a city'?"

"There is more in volunteering than I thought," Rob said, gravely, after a long pause; "I am afraid, after all, that I am one of the kind waiting for a draft."

"And, if you wait for that, you may be left out altogether. Rob, it is not very easy work to march and countermarch, to dig trenches, throw up earthworks, keep your eyes open and your senses keen through dreary night-watches and the many other duties that fill up a soldier's life. It is harder for some men to keep faithful to these than to go into battle and die covered with glory. But on the other side there will be a few questions asked. What was the man's life? I often think of what the Saviour said,—not be faithful *in* death, but be 'faithful *unto* death.' There, we have had quite a sermon. Next month you will be a new recruit, you know."

"Two games!" exclaimed Dick, as they advanced. "Each party has won one."

"And I am tired," said Ada, languidly.

"Just one more," pleaded Dick; "I know that I shall have better luck."

"I can't," Ada replied.

Rob's first impulse was to say, "I'll take her place"; but he felt that would leave Ada to her own resources again. He did not care anything about Ada's noticing him, — indeed, she rather ignored him when Dick was around; but he had a fancy that Dick was *his* friend, and did not belong so exclusively to the girls.

"Rob, I'll try you," Mr. Meredith exclaimed, remarking the wistful face.

So Ada and Dick had a ramble about the grounds, as Kathie, feeling she was not very earnestly desired, lingered to watch the players. It was a pretty sharp game, but Robert beat.

"Though I do not think you played your best at the last," the boy said.

Uncle Edward gave a queer little smile that set Rob to musing. What if people sometimes acted a little differently, for the sake of sparing his unlucky temper!

"I shall have to fight giants," he confessed to himself, understanding, as he never had before, how serious a warfare life really is.

Dick could not be persuaded to remain to supper, though Ada made herself very charming. But they passed a pleasant evening without him. Indeed, it seemed to Rob that there was some new element in their enjoyment. Was it because Ada was more gracious than usual?

Uncle Robert could have told the secret easily.

"Don't you get dreadfully dull sometimes?" Ada asked as they were alone in their room, for Ada had chosen to share Kathie's.

"Dull!" and Kathie gave her pleasant little laugh.

"When there is no company? For it is not quite like the city, where one can have calls and evening amusements."

"I hardly ever think of it. You know I was not here last winter, and the summer has been so very delightful!" Kathie's cheeks glowed at the remembrance.

" But your brother will be away this coming winter."

" Yes." It would make some difference, to be sure, but Kathie fancied that she should not be entirely miserable.

" If I were you, I should want to go to boarding-school. Where there is a crowd of girls they always manage to have a nice time."

" But I have nice times at home. I do not want to go away."

" What a queer girl you are, Kathie ! "

It was not the first time she had been called queer. But she said, rather gayly, " In what respect ? "

" I should n't like to do as you have to. Why, there are five servants in our house, and only one in this great place ! And we have only four children, while your mother has three. It is hardly fair for you to be compelled to do so much work when there is no necessity."

" Mamma thinks it best," Kathie answered.

" If you expected to be very poor — or would have to do housework — "

" I might," returned Kathie, pleasantly. " People are sick sometimes, and servants go away."

"Is n't your uncle willing that you should have a chambermaid?"

"I suppose he would be if mamma desired it."

"So you have to keep your own room in order, and dust the parlor, and do all manner of little odds and ends. I believe I saw you wiping some dishes in the kitchen this morning."

"And it did not injure me," returned Kathie, laughingly.

"But all this work makes your hands hard and red. Mine are as soft as satin. I believe no money would tempt me to sweep a room!"

Ada uttered this in a very lofty fashion.

"Mamma thinks it best for me to learn to do everything. She was brought up in a good deal of luxury, but met with reverses afterward."

Kathie smiled inwardly at the picture she remembered of the little room where her mother used to sit and sew, and how *she* did errands, swept, washed dishes, and sometimes even scrubbed floors. Her hands were not large or coarse, for all the work they had done.

"I think it would be hard enough if one was compelled to do it. I am thankful that I have no taste

for such menial employments. I do not believe that
I could even toast a piece of bread"; and Ada leaned
back in the low rocker, the very picture of complacency.

Kathie was silent, revolving several matters in her
mind "all in a jumble," as she would have said.
She knew it would be useless to undertake to explain
to Ada the great difference between their lives.
Mamma, Aunt Ruth, and Uncle Robert believed in
the great responsibility of existence. Weeks, months,
and years were not given to be squandered away in
frivolous amusement. To do for each other was one
of the first conditions, not merely the small family
circle, but all the wide world outside who needed
help or sympathy. And if one did not know how to
do anything —

"But when you go to school you cannot do so
much," pursued Ada. "There will be all your lessons. I suppose you will study French and Italian
You cannot think how I was complimented on my
singing while I was at Saratoga. Several gentlemen
said my pronunciation was wonderful in one so young.
I hope I shall be able to come out next summer."

"Come out!" repeated Kathie, bewildered.

"Yes, be regularly introduced to society. I am past fifteen, and growing tall rapidly. I hope I shall have an elegant figure. I want to be a belle. Don't you suppose you shall ever go to Saratoga?"

"I don't know," — dubiously.

"It would be a shame for you to grow up here where there is no society. You would surely be an old maid, like your Aunt Ruth."

"She is n't so very old," returned Kathie, warmly.

"But every woman over twenty-five is an old maid. I mean to be married when I am eighteen."

Kathie brushed out her hair, hung up her clothes, and waited for Ada to get into bed so that she might say her prayers in peace. Ada had outgrown "Our Father which art in heaven," and "had no knack of making up prayers," she said.

But it seemed to Kathie that there were always so many things for which to give thanks, so many fresh blessings to ask. She almost wondered a little, sometimes, if God did n't get tired of listening.

CHAPTER II.

DRAFTED.

Miss Jessie smiled a little at Ada's assumption of womanhood when the two girls came over to drink tea.

"Ah," said Grandmother Darrell, wiping her glasses, "she's no such a girl as Kathie! The child's worth half a dozen of her. After all, there's no place like the country to bring up boys and girls."

For Grandmother Darrell, like a good many other people, fancied everything that came from the city must be more or less contaminated.

"I think Miss Darrell *would* make your uncle a very nice wife," Ada said, graciously. "Do you suppose there is anything in it?"

Kathie flushed scarlet, remembering the pain and trouble of last winter. "I don't want to talk about it," she answered, in a low tone.

Ada nodded her head sagaciously. It was quite evident that she had hit upon the truth.

Some of the Brookside girls thought Ada " so splendid," Lottie Thorne among them, who now treated Kathie in a very amiable manner, and always took pains to speak with her as they came out of church. Of course, Lottie was growing older and a little more sensible, as well as worldly wise.

They took Ada to all the pleasant haunts, rowed over the lake, made two or three visits, and Mrs. Alston invited some girls, or rather young ladies, to tea; but Ada showed a decided preference for the young gentlemen. Even unsuspicious Kathie remarked how soon her headaches disappeared, and how ready she was to sing if some of the boys would stand at the piano and turn her music.

" A budding coquette," said Aunt Ruth, with a quiet smile.

" What a pity that girls should be reared to such idle, frivolous lives, and have their minds so filled with vanity and selfishness!" Mrs. Alston replied. " Can such blossoming bring forth good, wholesome fruit ? "

Mr. Meredith felt a little annoyed. The visit was not quite the success he had hoped, and he saw more clearly than ever the difference between the two girls; but ah, how unlike their mothers were!

Was he growing more serious, clearer - eyed? What was there about this family that charmed so insensibly? The higher motives, the worthier lives, with a more generous outlook for neighbor and friend!

Kathie was ashamed to confess it even to herself, but she said good by at the station with a sense of relief. For days a horrible thought had been haunting her, — suppose Uncle Robert *should* be drafted! The abruptly terminated conversation had not been renewed; indeed, there had been so many pleasures at Cedarwood that one hardly wanted to bring in such a subject. But if it did happen, Kathie felt she should want no· stranger eyes to witness her grief.

For when the question came directly home, she felt that she could not give him up; yet how brave she had been last winter! If General Mackenzie could look into her heart, he would find that she hardly deserved all his praise.

But all Brookside was much excited over the prospect. Business was very dull and bounties tempting; so numbers enlisted.

"Uncle Robert," Kathie said, as they were riding homeward, "could a drafted man offer a substitute just the same?"

"Why, yes, to be sure."

He uttered the words in such a light-hearted manner that she felt quite relieved, but lacked courage to pursue the subject further. A little quiver would keep rising from her heart to her throat, interfering with the steadiness of her voice.

By Monday night seventy men were still needed to complete the quota. That gave Brookside about forty.

Kathie wondered how they could all go on with their usual routine. Aunt Ruth, even, sat by the window and sang "Bonnie Doon," as she sewed upon Rob's outfit. His uncle had decided upon a school about sixty miles distant, a flourishing collegiate institution, in a healthy locality, — a quaint, quiet, old-fashioned town, with a river where the boys could have boating and swimming.

"It is so far!" Mrs. Alston had said at first.

"Not too far, though. Of course we do not expect him to come home every few weeks. That always unsettles a boy."

So she made no further demur. The principal, Dr. Goldthwaite, was a truly religious man, and the place was held in high esteem. Perhaps this took their thoughts a little from the subject that was so absorbing to Kathie.

Rob went over to the hall and hung about all the morning. He did find a good deal of amusement in it. The crowd was disposed to be rather jolly, and several of the men took their luck with great good-humor. It was as his uncle had said. While they would not willingly leave their homes and families, still, if the country had need of them in her imminent peril, they would go. Others, sure of a substitute, took the news with unconcern. Only a few exhibited any anger, or declared loudly what they would and what they would not do.

At three o'clock the printed list was complete, and the notices were being made up.

"So your uncle 's in for it, Rob!" exclaimed a voice at his side.

"No, you 're mistaken. I listened to every name."

"Here it is, — Robert Conover !"

Rob followed the grimy finger down the list. Sure enough ! His heart stood still for a moment.

" He will get a sub, though!   He 'd be a fool to go
when he 's rich enough to stay at home!"

" Yes, that 's it!" and a burly fellow turned,
facing them with a savage frown.   " It 's the poor
man this 'ere thing comes hard on!   Rich men are
all   cowards!   They kin stay to hum and nuss
themselves in the chimbly-corner.   I say they 're
cowards!"

Rob's heart swelled within him for a twofold
reason.   First, the shock.   He had not been able to
believe that the draft would touch them, and the
surprise was very great.   Then to have his uncle
called a coward!   All the boy's hot, unreasoning
indignation was ablaze.

" He is not!" he answered, fiercely.

" Say that agin and I 'll knock you over!"

Rob was not to be dared or to be bullied into
silence.   He stood his ground manfully.

" I say that my uncle is no coward, whether he
gets a substitute or not!"

The fellow squared off.   It was Kit Kent, as he
was commonly called, a blacksmith of notoriously
unsteady habits.

" None of that!" and a form was interposed between Rob and his assailant. "Hit a fellow of your size, Kent, not a boy like that."

"Let the youngster hold his tongue then! Much he knows!"

Rob did not stir, but his lips turned blue and almost cold with the pressure. If he had been a little larger, it seemed to him that he could not have let Kent alone.

"There 's a chance for you to make some money," exclaimed a voice in the crowd. "Six or seven hundred dollars, and you 're grumbling about being out of work! It 's a golden opportunity, and you 'll never find another like it."

That turned the laugh upon Kent. Rob walked off presently. Turning into a quiet street, he nearly ran over two men who stood talking.

"The trouble is that you can hardly find a substitute. Most of the able-bodied men who will go have enlisted or been drafted. The look is mighty poor!"

That startled Rob again. He began to feel pretty sober now. What if —

Kathie and Aunt Ruth had gone out into the garden, and were taking up some flowers for winter.

"O Rob!" exclaimed Kathie, with a cry, "is there

any news ? It's the worst, I know," answering her own question, her breath almost strangling her.

"Yes, it is the worst !"

"Uncle Robert has been drafted!" Kathie dropped her trowel and flew to her mother. " But he won't go," she sobbed ; "do you think he will ? How can we spare him ? "

"It would be no worse for us than for hundreds of others," replied her mother. " Kathie, my darling, be brave until we know, at least."

" Where is he ? "

" He went to Connor's Point with Mr. Langdon. Hush, dear, don't cry."

Kathie wiped away her tears. " It is very hard," she said. " I never realized before how hard it was."

But the flowers lost their charm. Kathie put away her implements, laid off her garden-dress, as she called it, — a warm woollen sack and skirt, — and sat down, disconsolately enough, to practise her music. Next week she was going to school.

She heard Uncle Robert's voice on the porch at the side entrance. Rob was talking in great earnest ; but somehow she could n't have gone out, or trusted the voice still so full of tears.

He came in at length. "You have heard the news, Kitty?"

She rose and went to his arms, hid her face upon his shoulder. "O Uncle Robert!"

"What ought I to do, little one?"

It was such a solemn question that she could not answer it readily, selfishly.

"Rob came very near getting into a row on my behalf. It was rather funny. Poor boy! I believe he would go willingly in my stead."

The story interested Kathie a good deal, and turned the current of her feelings somewhat. Then one or two of the neighbors came in, and they had no more quiet until they gathered round the supper-table. Freddy thought it a great honor to be drafted.

"Is it true that there is a scarcity of substitutes?" asked Rob of his uncle.

"I believe it is. Mr. Langdon put in one about a month ago, and paid a thousand dollars."

"But you could afford that," said Rob, decisively.

"What about the cowardice of the proceeding?"

Rob colored. The matter appeared so different to him now.

"O Uncle Robert!"— in a most deprecating tone.

"I will not perplex you, nor keep you in suspense," he said, gravely. "If your father was alive I think I should not hesitate a moment. The country is at her sorest need, and calls upon her loyal children for assistance. It is the duty of every man who can be spared to answer the call, to swell the list so that the struggle may be brief. It seems to me that another year will certainly see our war ended, now that we have such brave and able generals in the field, but if the stress should be any greater, I *must* respond. Now, however, I shall do my best to procure a substitute."

They all drew a relieved breath. Kathie looked up with a tender light in her eyes.

"I am so glad!" she said afterward, nestling beside him upon the sofa. "Did it surprise you when you heard that you were drafted?"

"I must confess that it did. I had a presentiment that I should escape, so it seems such things are not always to be depended upon."

Kathie was silent for some time, her eyes engrossed with a figure in the carpet.

"Well, Miss Thoughtful, what is it now? Are you not satisfied to have me stay, or am I less of a hero in your eyes?"

"No, Uncle Robert. I was only thinking of the men who were compelled to go and did not want to, who had families to leave —"

"My darling, it is not necessary to lay the cares of others so deeply to heart. Instead, we must do all we can for those who are left behind."

"I don't think a draft quite a fair thing, after all," declared Rob, coming out of a brown study.

Mrs. Alston entered the room. "Mr. Morrison is over here and wishes to see you, — Ethel's father."

Uncle Robert rose and went out.

In the mean while Aunt Ruth and Rob had quite a warm discussion concerning the draft. Kathie somehow felt very tender-hearted, and was silent.

Presently they heard steps in the hall and the door opened.

"I have brought Mr. Morrison in to see you all," Mr. Conover said, "and to explain to you that he desires to go in my stead, a willing substitute."

There was something very solemn and withal sweet in Uncle Robert's voice. Rob winked away a tear. Kathie walked over to Mr. Morrison and laid her hand in his, — a pretty white hand if she did dust the rooms and do gardening with it.

"It is so very kind and generous in you," she began, falteringly, thinking of another love and another substitute.

"No, Miss Kathie, it is n't all pure generosity, so don't praise me too soon. If I 'd been real lucky about getting work, maybe I should n't have taken the idea so strongly into my mind, or if poor Ethel's mother had lived. But times are unsettled, and business of all kinds is so very dull that I 'd half made up my mind to 'list and get the bounty. That would be something for my little girl in case she did n't have me. Then when I heard talk of the draft I thought to myself, 'If Mr. Conover gets taken I 'll offer to go in his place'; and so I waited. Being an Englishman, I am not liable, you know."

"And that makes it the more noble," returned Kathie, softly. "It was so good to — to think of him"; and her voice sank to a whisper.

"You have all been so kind to my poor old mother, and to me, for that matter, as well. I seem to owe some sort of duty to you first."

"Did you mean to enlist any way?" asked Kathie.

"Yes, miss, it would have come to that; for, said

I, 'Here is a country and a government battling in a good cause, begging for men, and willing to provide for the little ones they may leave behind.' Though I should be no skulk, nor eye-server, Miss Kathie, if I did go for the money."

"We should never think that of you," returned Uncle Robert, warmly.

"So I 'll be glad to go in your place, sir, if it 's any favor; and if you 'll look after Ethel a little, if anything should happen to me. If I 'm too bold in asking — "

"No," said Aunt Ruth; "it will be a sacred duty, and a pleasure as well; but we shall count upon your return."

"Life is uncertain with us all," was the grave reply. With that he rose and bowed. Uncle Robert left the room with him, for he had much more to say.

"I could n't have uttered a word," exclaimed Rob, his voice still a little tremulous. "Why, it 's just like a dream! There are noble and heroic men who may go to war even for the money, though I think they are a good deal sneered at, — subs, as the boys call them; but I shall never ridicule them again, — never, although bad men may do the same thing."

"It is not quite the same," subjoined Kathie.

"No, the motive makes a great difference."

Uncle Robert returned and took his seat between the children. He appeared to be invested with a new virtue in their eyes, as if he had just escaped an imminent and deadly peril. And there is something in the simplest act of chivalry that touches one's soul.

"It was so good in Mr. Morrison to think of you," Rob said, after a while.

"Yes; going farther back, I don't know but we owe it all to Kathie. If she had not thought of our trusty and efficient gardener, we should never have known his brother. The lodge has made a charming home for them, and they feel deeply grateful."

"It is worse to go away to war than I imagined," Rob continued, gravely following out his own musings.

"You have been looking at the glory and listening to the music, my boy; but there is quite another side to it. It is one thing to go out as a mounted officer, in glittering uniform, with a servant to wait upon you, and if you fall in battle to have whole cities weep your loss, and quite another to tramp as

a commom soldier, often weary and footsore, to be
subject to the caprice of those in authority, to work
night and day sometimes, to stand in the front rank
and be swept down by a terrific charge, be trampled
under foot and thrown into a nameless grave, perhaps forever lost to your kindred. It is no light
matter, Rob, and requires a good deal of courage
when a man does it intelligently."

"You would n't have gone out as a private,
though!"

A grave smile crossed Uncle Robert's face. "I
should not have gone for the glory, but the duty.
Yes, Rob, I should have taken my place in the ranks,
and if the great Captain of all had said, 'Friend,
come up higher,' I should have trusted through
his grace to be ready for the promotion. But one
goes in my stead."

Kathie thought of the One who had gone in the
place of us all, been mocked, derided, spit upon, and
put to a cruel death. Maybe the rest remembered it
too, for there was no more talking. Their hearts
were too full.

CHAPTER III.

TRUE TO ONE'S COLORS.

THERE was a week of great excitement at Brook-side. Head-quarters were established on the confines of the town to render it accessible to Taunton and the adjacent places. Hundreds thronged the camp daily; uniforms were sent down, and drilling commenced in good earnest.

Kathie began school on Monday morning. A large, pleasant room had been obtained, and Mrs. Wilder opened with ten young ladies, though nearly as many more had been enrolled.

"I feel as if I were drafted," she declared to Uncle Robert. "I know it is my duty to go and do the best that I can, but I would so much rather have remained at home."

"You find, then, that no one is quite exempt from the warfare?" and he smiled. "Still, I think I can trust you to be a good soldier."

"I am second in the regiment," she said. "Mr. Morrison must always stand first."

It seemed very quiet and lonesome in that large room, where you were put upon your honor not to speak, and the silence was broken only by the recitations, or some remark of Mrs. Wilder. A long, dull day, though the session closed at two, there being no intermission.

Lottie Thorne was the only girl Kathie was well acquainted with. That ambitious young lady had pleaded very hard for boarding-school, and, being disappointed, was rather captious and critical. Emma Lauriston sat next to her, and Kathie fancied she might like her very much. She had met her in the summer at the rowing-matches.

But she was glad enough to get home. Rob had his head full of Camp Schuyler, and Freddy had arrayed himself in gorgeous regimentals and sat out on a post drumming fearfully.

"I want a little more talk about this substitute business," said Uncle Robert, at the table. "Mr. Morrison offered to go for seven hundred dollars. He has three hundred of his own. Now what do you think we ought to give him?"

He addressed the question more particularly to Rob and Kathie.

Rob considered. In his boy's way of thinking he supposed what any one asked was enough.

"Would a thousand dollars be too much ?" Kathie ventured, timidly. "It does n't seem to me that any money could make up to Ethel for — "

There Kathie stopped.

"He will come back," exclaimed Rob.

"We were talking over Ethel's future this morning. Mr. Morrison would like to have her educated for a teacher. I am to be appointed her guardian in case of any misfortune."

"It ought not to be less than a thousand," said Aunt Ruth.

"I thought so myself. And I believe I shall pledge my word to provide a home for Ethel in case of any change at her uncle's."

Kathie's deep, soft eyes thanked him.

The next day the bargain was concluded. Mr. Morrison handed his small sum over to Mr. Conover for safe-keeping, and the whole amount, thirteen hundred dollars, was placed at interest. Then he re-ported himself at Camp Schuyler for duty.

Kathie tried bravely to like her school, but home was so much dearer and sweeter. It was quite hard after her desultory life, and spasmodic studying made so very entertaining by Uncle Robert's explanations, to come down to methodical habits and details. She meant to be a good soldier, even if it did prove difficult in the early marches.

But this week was one of events. On Thursday afternoon Mr. Meredith surprised them all again. It seemed to Kathie that there was something unusual in his face. Uncle Robert was absent on important business, and at first he appeared rather disappointed.

"It is such a glorious afternoon, Kitty, that I think you will have to invite me out to drive, by way of comfort. Are the ponies in good order?"

"Yes, and at home. How fortunate that Rob did not take them!"

Kathie ordered them at once.

"You have had great doings here. So you came near losing your dear uncle, my child?"

Kathie winked away a tear. There would always be a tender little spot in her heart concerning the matter.

"It is best under the circumstances," was Mr. Meredith's grave comment. "I should not want him to go."

They took their seats in the phaeton. "Where shall we drive?" Kathie asked. "To —" breaking off her sentence with a little blush.

"Miss Darrell is away from home. It is owing to that circumstance that you are called upon to entertain me"; and he laughed a little, but less gayly than usual.

It was a soft, lovely autumn day, full of whisperings of oaks and pines and cedars, fragmentary chirps of birds, and distant river music. Kathie drew a few long breaths of perfect content, then with her usual consideration for others she stole a shy glance to see if Mr. Meredith was enjoying it as well, he was so very quiet.

"I am afraid something troubles you," she said, softly; and her voice sounded as if it might have been a rustle of maple branches close at hand. "Is it about Uncle Robert?"

"No, child," in a grave, reflective tone; "it is — about myself."

She did not like to question him as she would have done with Uncle Robert.

"Kitten," he began, presently, "I have been thinking this good while, and thinking slowly. A great many things puzzle me, and all my perplexities have culminated at last in one grand step; but whether I am quite prepared for it —"

The sentence was a labyrinth to Kathie, and she was not quite sure that she held the clew.

"I am going to enlist — at least, I am going out for three months — with my regiment. They have volunteered, most of them."

"And what troubles you?" in her sweet, tender voice, and glancing up with an expression that no other eyes save Kathie Alston's could have had.

"Child," he asked, "how did you stand fire last winter when you were so suddenly brought to the front? About the singing, I mean."

She understood. He referred to the Sunday evening at Mrs. Meredith's when she had refused to join Ada in singing songs. The remembered pain still made her shiver.

"There is something about you, Kathie, just a little different from other children, — other girls. You often carry it in your face; and for the life of me I cannot help thinking how the wise virgins must have been illuminated with their tiny lamps while the others stood in darkness. Is it a natural gift or grace?"

She knew now what he meant. She was called upon to give testimony here, and it was almost as hard as in Mrs. Meredith's grand drawing-room. She felt the warm blood throbbing through every pulse.

"You did a brave thing that night, little girl. I shall never forget it — never. *Can* you answer my question? What *is* it?"

She could only think of one thing, one sentence, amid the whirl and confusion of ideas and the girlish shrinking back, — "The love of Christ constraineth us."

"It was n't merely your regard for your mother or Uncle Robert?"

"It was *all*," — in her simple, earnest fashion.

"I 'm going out there, Kathie," nodding his head southward, "to stand some pretty hard fire, doubtless. I am not afraid of physical pain, nor the dropping out of life, though existence never was sweeter than now; but if, in the other country, the record of my useless years rises sharp against me, what shall I answer? I have never tried to do anything for the glory of God! Child, you shame all our paltry lives!"

" O, don't ! " with a suggestion of pain in her voice ; " what I can do is such a very little."

She would never know how the simple acts of her life, springing from the hidden centre that was deeper even than her every-day thought, was to bear fruit on wide-spread branches.

" And yet we — I — do nothing. I should have to go empty-handed."

She cast about for some words of comfort. As girl or woman Kathie Alston would never be able to realize all the frivolousness, to say nothing of vanity, selfishness, and deeper sins, crowded into this man's life, which still looked so fair by outward comparison with others.

" Ever since Mr. Morrison offered to go in Uncle Robert's place this verse has been lingering in my mind : ' Greater love hath no man than this, that a man lay down his life for his friends.' It seems to me that it does n't mean physical life altogether, but all the times and places when we take something precious out of our own lives and put it into that of others. And every man who goes now may be called upon to suffer in some other's stead. If he do it bravely, is it not a little of the good fruit ? I can't

4

explain all I mean, only just as the Saviour loved us we ought to love every one else."

Edward Meredith had listened to many an eloquent sermon, and dissected it in a purely intellectual fashion, his heart never warming with any inward grace, or hungering after the true bread. But he understood now the secret of this little girl's life. Not doctrine, not so much creed, or form, or rule, "but the taking something precious out of her daily existence and noiselessly placing it in that of others." And the same love which enabled her to do this rendered her brave, pure, and sweet. A child's religion, that a year or two ago he would have sneered at, and now he had come to learn of her because he was too proud to ask others, and perhaps ashamed.

"But you had a substitute!" she said, presently, bethinking herself.

"Yes. He has served his time out honorably, has had the good fortune to come home without harm of any kind. You remember how Mackenzie bantered me last winter, though he was in dead earnest. But the country is at her extremest need now; if Grant, Sherman, and our other generals, are strengthened by good reinforcements, it seems to me that in six months we might have peace. I have done a good deal of holiday soldiering in my life, but this is to be sober earnest."

He looked as if it might be.

"When will you go?"

"We start for Washington on Saturday morning."

"So soon! Does — Miss Jessie know?" Kathie could not help but ask it, though the lids trembled over her shy, downcast eyes.

"She should have received my note this morning. I suppose she did not, or she would have been at home. Kathie, I ought to thank you for your rare delicacy in keeping our secret. There are some matters that one does not like to have talked about."

What would Miss Jessie say? Of course she loved Mr. Meredith very much. Kathie's heart ached a little in silence, but this was one of the burdens that could not be borne by another.

On they went through lovely scenery, now and then catching a glimpse of the river that wound around like a silver cord through its bed of green. Here in the stillness they heard the chatter of squirrels and the sound of dropping nuts, or an autumntinted leaf went floating on the air like some gorgeous bird with his wings all aflame. Golden-rod and great clumps of purple Michaelmas daisies starred the roadside, **with frequent** clusters of scarlet sumach, **pendent** bitter-sweet berries with the still glossy **green leaves, and** the dark tint of spruce and fir.

Kathie began to realize how her heart and intellect had expanded. She was no longer a little girl. **How she had grown** within and without **was a** great mystery, as well as how her soul had enriched itself **with** drawing near to others, and going forth again with **the** sweet, half-comprehending sympathies **of** girlhood.

"I have been a dull companion," Mr. Meredith said, at length. "**But, Kathie, I shall never forget** the happy days **I** have spent at Cedarwood. To have known you is one of the bright events in my **life.**"

They were coming up the avenue, and saw Uncle Robert standing on the broad porch. **She might** never have another opportunity to speak, and he **had** been so peculiarly serious this afternoon.

"**O Mr.** Meredith, you won't forget — when you are out there — that **there is** another service, and another Captain — "

"Pray for me, Kathie, that I may be one of His faithful soldiers to my life's end."

She ran up stairs afterward, and the two gentlemen had a long talk in the library. After supper Mr. Meredith said good by, as he expected to leave the Darrells' to take the early morning train.

"I do believe everybody is going to war!" exclaimed Rob, rather ruefully. "I wonder if we shall ever have such good times again."

Rob spent the next forenoon in packing.

"How all these things are to be gotten into one trunk I cannot imagine!" he exclaimed, in despair.

"I fancy that you had better put the clothes in first, and leave the 'things,' as you call them, until the last," said Aunt Ruth, with a quiet smile.

"But I shall want them all, I 'm sure."

"Not your whole tool-chest!"

"Some of the articles would come in so handy."

"To assist you in learning your lessons?" asked his mother.

"O, you know what I mean. Now, mother, you won't let Freddy meddle with them while I am gone,

— will you? He always does manage to get into everything."

"The best way will be to put all that you can in the closet of your play-room, and give Uncle Robert the key. Lock all your drawers as well."

One would have fancied that Rob was going to Europe, to say the very least. After he had tumbled the articles in and out about twenty times, he concluded that he would go down to the stable to see about some trifle.

So his mother soon had the trunk in order, though she quietly restored half the "traps" to their place in the play-room, and I doubt if Rob ever missed them.

Saturday was another very busy time with him. He had to take a farewell glimpse of Camp Schuyler, to visit hosts of the boys, to take a last row, a last ride, a last game of ball, and one might have imagined from all these preparations that he was about to enter a dungeon and leave the cheerful ways of life behind.

But Rob was beginning to have quite serious moods occasionally; and the last Sunday at home was one of them. He did not feel nor understand the

transition state as keenly as Kathie, he was such
a thorough, careless, rollicking boy. He would play
until the last gasp, — "until whiskers began to
sprout," he said, — and he would make one of the
men to whom recollections of boyish fun would
always be sweet.

The sermon in the morning touched him a little,
and then the talk with Charlie Darrell. The Darrells felt very badly over the present loss of their
dear friend; and Kathie just pressed Miss Jessie's
fingers, but spoke no word.

"I do mean to *try*," Rob said, that evening, to
Kathie. "It seems almost as if I were really going
to war, as well as the rest of them."

"Yes," she answered, gravely; "you will find
enough fighting to do, — foes without and within."

"I have learned some things, though," — with a
confident nod, — "and I shall never forget about the
giants. What odd times we have had, Kathie, from
first to last!"

"I wonder if you will be homesick?"

"Pshaw! No. A great boy like me! No doubt
there 'll be lots of fun."

"But I hope you will not get into any troubles or scrapes. O Rob! it is real difficult to always do just what is right, when oftentimes wrong things seem so much pleasanter."

"I wonder why it is, Kathie? It always looked rather hard to me. Why did n't God make the wrong so that you could see it plainly?"

"If we see it, that is sufficient. Maybe if we kept looking at it steadily it would grow larger; but you know we often turn to the pleasant side when we should be watching the danger."

"I don't believe that I can ever be real good; but I 'll never tell a lie, nor be mean, nor shirk, nor cheat! I want to be a real splendid man like Mr. Meredith!"

Rob would never outgrow that boyish admiration. Edward Meredith would have felt a good deal humbled if he had known how this boy magnified some of his easy-going ways into virtues.

They had a sweet, sad time singing in the evening. Kathie had begun to play very nicely, with a great deal of expression and tenderness; and to-night all the breaks, all the farewells, and the loneliness to come, seemed to be struggling in her soul.

She was glad that no one saw her face, for now and then a tear dropped unbidden.

Rob and his mother had their last talk at bed-time. Her heart was sad enough at the thought of the nine months' absence, for at Westbury there were no short vacations. True, she would have the privilege of visiting him, but such interviews must, of necessity, be brief.

He lay awake a long while, thinking and resolv-ing. How many times he had "tried to be good." Why could n't he remember? What was it that helped his mother, and Uncle Robert, and Kathie? The grace of God; but then how was one to get this grace?

Wandering off into the fields of theology, Rob fell asleep, and never had another thought until the breakfast-bell rang. Then, as he recalled his per-plexity, he said slowly to himself, "I don't believe religion comes natural to boys."

The parting was sad, after all. A thousand thoughts rushed into his mind. What if he should be homesick? Here was the roomy playhouse, with its store of tools, books in abundance, the ponies, the lake, the boys, — O, everything! and Rob's fast-coming breath was one great sob.

"A good soldier," Kathie whispered, as his arms were round her neck.

Uncle Robert did not return until the next day. The accounts were very encouraging. Clifton Hall had taken Rob's fancy at once. The boys were coming in on Monday; so there was little done beside fraternizing and being classified and shown to their dormitories. He had written a little scrap of a note stating that "everything was lovely."

They missed him very much. Kathie began to wonder if *her* winter would n't be lonesome. No gay Mr. Meredith to drop in upon them now and then; no noisy, merry boys such as had haunted the grounds all summer. She began to feel sadly disconsolate.

But she rallied presently. "I must fight as well as my soldiers," she said to herself.

The next event was Mr. Morrison's departure. Uncle Robert took both families over the day they "broke camp."

Mr. Morrison wrung Uncle Robert's hand warmly. "It will be all right, whatever comes," he said. "If I had not gone for you I should have done it for some one else, so never give yourself an anxious thought about it. I know my little lass is in good hands."

. He kissed Ethel many, many times, and she clung to him with an almost breaking heart. Kathie's quick eyes saw a duty here.

CHAPTER IV.

LITTLE STEPS BY THE WAY.

BUT Kathie found that the regiment's marching off to Virginia had not taken all the interest of life. They had left the woods behind, glowing with rich autumnal coloring, the glorious blue heavens, the ripening fruits, and the changeful scenes, that opened afresh every day.

Her afternoons were quite a delight. Uncle Robert always held himself in readiness, and they had either a ride or a ramble. There were new collections of ferns to make, and with these she often had an entertaining lesson in botany.

October was very pleasant indeed. There was no frost to mention until the middle of the month, and by that time the flowers were safely housed. Hugh Morrison had built a conservatory against the south side of the barn, and promised Kathie bouquets all winter.

Kathie began to look up her old friends as well,

and she joined the girls in several nutting expeditions, at which they had rare fun.

Withal she had a brief note from Ada, who wondered if she approved the foolish step Uncle Edward had taken. Papa was positively angry about it! And then the idea of going out as a private, even if it was in a "crack" regiment. However, they really did n't mean to fight, and that was some comfort. He would be at home by the first of January.

But General Grant evinced no desire to go into winter quarters, while at the South and West there was unusual activity.

"It looks as if there might be considerable fighting before Christmas!" declared Uncle Robert.

For the few who chose to find them there were duties enough. Brookside, as well as other places, began to feel the effects of the war. There were soldiers' widows and orphans, the sick and the wounded who were sent home to make room for newer cases. Then the churches at Brookside decided to give a grand Fair and Festival for this benevolent object, to be held Thanksgiving week.

Kathie found her hands quite full. Still she found time to dust the parlor every morning and take care of her own room, and often managed to get half an hour for her music practice. To be sure, she did not dawdle over her dressing, neither was there a waterfall wonderfully constructed, and adorned with puffs and braids.

"I mean to keep my little girl simple in her tastes as long as I can," Mrs. Alston replied to the dress-maker. "Nothing can be prettier than her hair as it is, and I do not feel justified in dressing her expensively when there are so many children suffering with cold and hunger."

"But young girls feel so sensitive on these matters," was the reply. "They all want to look like their companions."

"I hope there are some sensible mothers left," returned Mrs. Alston with a smile.

Kathie was very much interested in getting contributions and making fancy articles, though hers tended rather to the useful. And Aunt Ruth, to her great amusement, made up a dozen stout gingham kitchen aprons with bibs, a stack of kettle-holders, and knitted some dishcloths out of soft cotton.

In the mean while Kathie was delighted with a letter from Mr. Meredith. He was in the gayest spirits and related a host of comical episodes. He had been in several skirmishes, but no regular battle, was well and hearty, and brown as a berry already. Just at the last he said, "I have not forgotten our pleasant ride, and the other fighting we talked about."

Mr. Morrison was doing very well also. Kathie began to think that it was not such a terrible thing to go to war, after all.

As for Rob, his record was pretty fair. He did confess to being a little homesick at first. The Latin was "awful tough work," and some of the rules "rather hard on a fellow who was new to them." But they had a "jolly set of boys," and he liked it first-rate.

So Kathie had no need to worry about her soldiers. She said a little prayer for them night and morning, and thought of them often. But she was so busy and so happy that she was little inclined to look upon the dark side.

The Fair was a decided success. It was held at Mason's Hall and opened on Monday evening. Emma Lauriston, and a number of the larger girls, were in attendance upon the tables. The band came up from Connor's Point and discoursed patriotic music. The hall was large, well lighted, and presented a very gay appearance.

But the most amusement was created by a " Dutch kitchen." Several ladies had transformed a small ante-room into a very attractive place of resort. There were great brown rafters overhead, from which depended hams, flitches of bacon, strings of onions, bunches of herbs, and at the edge were stowed away miscellaneous articles. A great eight-day clock, chairs, and an old brass-handled dresser that might have come over in the Mayflower, while four pretty young girls, in the quaint old costume of their grandmothers, waited upon the table with all grace and ease. This was crowned with an immense dish of beans and pork, and a stout, rosy Dutch woman was baking waffles. Altogether this was the place for fun.

Kathie had been in and out half a dozen times. Her Fortunatus's purse was full to repletion, and every time she passed the door she saw some children standing there with wistful eyes. It was such a delightful thing to make any one happy.

Sauntering round, she came to a rather oddly arranged table, — Miss Weston's. She was the primmest

and queerest of old maids, — a little body with weak
eyes and flaxen hair, who always looked at you
sharply through gold-bowed spectacles.

"O dear !" she exclaimed, "how you young things
do go flyin' round ! As for me, I 'm that tired I 'm
just ready to drop. I 've been here ever sence two
o'clock and never set down a minnit. I fixed all
my table myself, and I made nigh onto all the things.
Cousin Hitty, she sent me them there child's aperns ;
but land ! what a sight of folly it is to do all that
braidin' and nonsense ! I never had no sech thing
when I was little ! Been in the Dutch kitchen ? "

"O yes, time and again."

"I 'd like to go, I 'm sure. I 've been standin'
stiddy on my feet sence two o'clock. If some one
would come along and take my table !"

"Could n't I ? " asked Kathie.

"O, you 're so flighty ! All gals are nowadays.
Why, when I was no older 'n you I had seven
bed-quilts pieced, and had begun to lay by sheets and
pillow-slips, and had a dozen pairs of as han'some
hum-knit stockings as you 'd find in a day's
walk !"

Miss Weston really did look tired. Kathie was

5

debating whether she should not insist, though this was an out-of-the-way corner, and rather dull.

"Well, I guess I'll go. You won't be likely to sell anything; nothing much sells the first night, and I hain't no nonsense and flummery. Good useful articles, but nobody can see their virtue nowadays. It's the way of the world!" — a little spitefully. "All the prices are marked in plain figgers, and I won't have a thing undersold. O dear, I am a'most beat out."

"I'll do my best," said Kathie, sweetly.

After giving about a dozen more orders Miss Weston moved slowly away, though, truth to tell, she was more anxious to go than she appeared; and whom should she meet just at the entrance but Mr. Denslow, who paid the ten cents' admittance fee. Mr. Denslow, moreover, was a widower, and Miss Weston had not quite given up the hope that the bed-quilts and the stores of linen might some day be called into use.

Kathie took her place behind the table, and, when the moments began to hang heavy, ventured upon a few improvements. The passers-by just gave the place a glance, and preferred to go where there were some pretty girls or some fun. Kathie found it exceedingly dull.

At last Mary Cox spied her out. Charlie Darrell was escorting her round.

"Why, Miss Weston," he said, softly, "where 's your specs? And why is n't your hair done up in queer little puffs?"

"What an ugly table!" exclaimed Mary. "How did you come to take it?"

"Miss Weston was so tired."

"She is in the Dutch kitchen, desperately sweet upon Mr. Denslow. It 's so seldom that she gets a beau that you need n't expect her for the next hour. What a lovely time you will have waiting!"

Charlie would have been very well satisfied to stay and talk to Kathie, but Mary wanted the amusement of rambling round and laughing with every one; and though Kathie said, beseechingly, "Don't go!" Mary replied, "O, we must!" and the child was left alone again.

Down at the end of the hall they were having a merry time. She saw grave Emma Lauriston laughing, and Aunt Ruth was talking and smiling. Why did n't some one think of her?

"How much fur these caliker aperns?" asked a country woman.

Kathie roused a little at the question, and took her eyes from the entertaining circle.

"Half a dollar!"

"Half a dollar!"—in the utmost surprise. "Why, they ain't wuth it! Ain't more 'n two yards of caliker in 'em, and I kin buy jest sich for fifteen cents a yard."

"But the making," suggested Kathie.

"O, that was throwed in! Always is in char'table objects. Tell you what I 'll do,—give three shillin's apiece for two of 'em. It 's a good object."

Now Kathie knew that the calico could not be bought for less than eighteen cents a yard, which would give just one cent profit; besides, Miss Weston had charged her particularly not to undersell. "The table is not mine," she answered; "I am keeping it for a friend."

Perhaps the woman considered there was a better chance of bargain-making; at all events she lingered and haggled until Kathie grew nervous, and wished Miss Weston would come.

"Well, you 're dreadful dear,—that 's all I 've

got to say"; and the woman flounced off angrily. "It's just the way at these fairs and things; but you can't cheat me out of my eyes, char'ty or not." Then Kathie was left alone again.

Presently Harry Cox ran over. "We're having such fun, and Charlie sent me for you. There's no one here, so why can't you shut up shop?"

Kathie longed to very much. She might keep an eye on the table and have a little fun besides; but it would be deserting her post. No true soldier would do that. "I'm obliged to you, but I think I had better stay; Miss Weston will soon be here."

"She's an old humbug!"

The sights and sounds were so tantalizing! What was Miss Weston doing in the Dutch kitchen all this while?

At last a bit of good-fortune befell Kathie. Mr. and Mrs. Adams and Mr. Langdon came along. Mr. Langdon had been away from Brookside for several weeks, and had a host of questions to ask.

"But what are you doing over here? You look as if you had quarrelled with your neighbors, and gone off in disdain."

Kathie explained that it was not her table.

"Have you sold anything?"

"Not a penny's worth!"

"Then I must patronize you a little," declared Mrs. Adams.

She found a number of useful articles, and some that she could give away to her poor parishioners. Kathie was quite proud of the four dollars in the small cash-box.

At last she was relieved, and gave a great breath of thankfulness.

"Is that *all* you 've taken in?" asked Miss Weston, rather sharply. "Are you sure you 've been here all the time? But you never can find any one who will do for you as you do yourself."

"I did not have but one customer," returned Kathie, in justification; and she felt that Mrs. Adams had made her purchases from a sense of personal friendship.

"I might better 'a' stayed with my table," was the ungracious answer; and that was all the thanks Kathie received for her kind deed and the discomfort. But she solaced herself with the consciousness that a great many good deeds meet with no reward in this world. Miss Weston must certainly have had some pleasure, or she would not have stayed so long.

Kathie was glad to get back to her mother and Aunt Ruth. The great source of amusement over here was the confectionery table with packages of "gift" candy, each parcel of which contained a present, and some of them were exceedingly comical.

"We have had such fun!" exclaimed Mary. "You don't know what you have missed!"

But Charlie glanced up and met Kathie's eyes with a look that seemed to understand it all; and Miss Jessie said afterward, "I think you were very good to keep Miss Weston's table such a long while. I did n't know but she meant to spend the whole evening in the kitchen."

At ten o'clock they began to put everything in order for closing up. The evening had been a wonderful success, considering that it was the first. Kathie was full of delight and excitement, and declared that she did not feel a bit sleepy, though it was after eleven when she went to her room.

The sleepiness came the next morning. Lessons were rather dull work, and she counted the moments eagerly until school closed. At first she had half a mind to run over to the hall to see how matters were progressing.

" But then it will be so much gayer this evening," she thought to herself, "and I must study my lessons a little."

She had sufficient courage to refuse all entreaties, and walked home by herself, trying to recall several subjects on which she had not been very perfect to-day. Mrs. Wilder was a little indulgent, for she knew how much the Fair had engrossed their attention.

The house was very quiet, so Kathie studied and had a good long music practice before mamma and Aunt Ruth returned. But as they were planning at the supper-table Mrs. Alston said, "I would rather not have you go to-night, Kathie."

"O mamma, why?" — with a touch of entreaty in her voice.

"You were up late last night, and you will want to be there again on Wednesday evening. You certainly need a little rest between."

"But last evening was like — lost time to me, or pretty nearly. I stayed at Miss Weston's table in that dull corner for more than an hour, while the other girls were enjoying themselves."

" Was it really lost time ? " and a half-smile crossed Mrs. Alston's face.

Kathie bethought herself. " I suppose it ought not to have been, but it was very dull."

" Are you sorry that you did it ? "

" Why, no," — in a tone of faint surprise. " And yet she did not seem very much obliged to me. Not that I cared so much for the thanks," — rather hastily.

" I was glad to see you willing to give up that much of your pleasure. Miss Weston is peculiar, but she was very ready to help everybody all the afternoon, and had her pins, scissors, strings, tacks, and hammer always ready. She did a great deal of work."

" But what a pity she cannot be — "

· " Well," said Uncle Robert, filling the long pause.

" A little more gracious, I believe I was going to say, or not quite so 'queer.' "

" It is unfortunate, when Miss Weston is so good-hearted in the main. But then she always talks about the trouble she has taken, the hard work she has done, and really dims the grace of her kind deeds."

"I came very near doing it myself," admitted Kathie, quite soberly.

"I do not believe Kathie desired any extra indulgence to-night because she gave up hers last evening," exclaimed Uncle Robert, with that namelessly appreciative light in his eyes.

"O no, do not think that of me, mamma, only I should like to go to-night. All the girls are to be there."

"Three nights' dissipation in succession is rather too much for a little girl, unless there was an urgent necessity. You will enjoy Wednesday evening all the better for having had a rest."

Kathie entreated no further, but it was a great disappointment, the more so because it had come so unexpectedly. And it seemed to her that she felt rested and bright enough to keep awake until midnight. She had studied all her lessons too.

However, she kissed her mother cheerfully. Aunt Ruth was tired, and did not mean to go either.

"You might put me to bed," exclaimed Freddy, lingering in the sitting-room.

Kathie somehow could not feel generous all at once. The idea of nursing her disappointment awhile looked rather tempting.

"Why, I never do it now," she answered.

"No, you don't," — considerably aggrieved. "Nor ever tell me stories, either! And it's so lonesome since Rob went to school."

Kathie had a faint consciousness that *not* to think of herself would be the best thing she could do.

"And you never told me about the Fair, either!"

"Well, run up to bed, and I will come presently," she said, in her bright, pleasant way.

Freddy kissed Aunt Ruth and went off in high feather. It was quite like old times to sit beside him and talk, and Kathie was not a little amused by his questions, some of which were very wise for a little head, and others utterly absurd. Then came some very slow, wandering sentences, and Kathie knew then that dusky-robed Sleep was hovering about the wondering brain until it could wonder no more.

"Good night," — with a soft kiss.

Aunt Ruth was lying on the lounge, so she ran down to the drawing-room and had half an hour's study over some "accidentals," that had tried her patience sorely in the afternoon. Delightful and all as music was, how much hard labor and persistence it required!

But by and by she could play the troublesome part with her eyes shut, counting the time to every note.

"Mr. Lawrence cannot find any fault with that!" she commented inwardly.

So she went back to Aunt Ruth in a very sweet humor, and, drawing an ottoman to the side of the lounge, sat down with Aunt Ruth's arm around her neck.

The room looked so lovely in its soft light. The shadowy flowers and baskets of trailing vines in the great bay-window, the dusky pictures on the wall, and the crimson tint given by the furniture. It was so sweet and restful that Kathie felt like having a good talk, so she drew a long breath by way of inspiration.

"Aunt Ruth," she said, in a little perplexity, "why is it that a person is not always willing to try to do right first of all? One wishes to and does not in the same breath."

"I suppose that is the result of our imperfect natures; but it is good to have the desire even."

"Yet when one means to try — is trying — will it never come easy?"

" Do you not find it easier than you did two years ago ? "

" But I am older, and have more judgment."

" And a stronger will on the wrong side as well as on the right, beside many more temptations."

" You conquer some of them, though."

" Yet with every new state of life others spring up. Life is a continual warfare."

" And you never get perfect ! "

" Never in this life."

" It is discouraging, — is n't it, Aunt Ruth ? "

" Is it discouraging to eat when you are hungry ? "

" Why, no ! " — with a little laugh.

" It seems to me the conditions of spiritual life are not so very unlike the conditions of physical life. It is step by step in both. The food and the grace are sufficient for the day, but they will not last to-morrow, or for a month to come."

" Yet the grace was to be sufficient always," Kathie said, with some hesitation.

" And have you proved it otherwise ? " The voice was very sweet, and Aunt Ruth's tone almost insensibly lured to confidence.

" But what troubles me is — that little things — "

and Kathie's voice seemed to get tangled up with emotion, "should be such a trial sometimes. Now I can understand how any great sacrifice may call for a great effort; but after we have been used to doing these little things over and over again —"

"One becomes rather tired of making the effort; and it is just here where so many people who mean to be good go astray. They leave the small matters to take care of themselves, and aspire to something greater; so, without being really aware of it, they are impatient, selfish, thoughtless for others, and fall into many careless ways. Would one really grand action make amends for all?"

"No, it would not," Kathie answered, reflectively.

"So we have to keep a watch every moment, be fed every day and hour, or we shall hunger."

Kathie sighed a little. Why had it not been as easy to be good and pleasant to-night as some other times when mamma did not think a coveted indulgence necessary? Yet her perplexity appeared so trivial that she hardly had the courage to confess it even to this kind listener.

"You took the right step to-night, Kathie," said Aunt Ruth, presently. "I was glad to see you do it.

Brooding over any real or fancied burden never lightens it. And though it seems a rather sharp remedy in the midst of one's pain to think of or help some other person, it works the speediest cure."

She saw that. So little a thing as entertaining Freddy had soothed her own disappointment.

"But I ought not —" and Kathie's voice trembled.

"Stoicism is not the highest courage, little one. And God does n't take away our natural feelings when he forgives sin. There is a good deal of sifting and winnowing left for us to do. And I believe God is better pleased with us when we have seen the danger, and struggled against it, than if it had not touched us at all. The rustle of the leaves seems to give promise of fruit."

"I think I see," Kathie answered, slowly. "There is some marching as well as all battle."

"Yes"; and Aunt Ruth kissed the tremulous scarlet lips.

Kathie was so soundly asleep that she did not hear mamma and Uncle Robert come home. But she was bright and winsome as a bird the next morning.

CHAPTER V.

ONE OF THE SMALL DEEDS.

KATHIE'S lessons, even to her music, were perfect the next day. Indeed, Mr. Lawrence quite complimented her.

Mrs. Alston said, " Kathie, if you would like to come over after school and relieve me a little while, I should be very glad."

So Kathie went straight from school. There was quite a crowd already. Whole families had come in from the country, farmers with their wives and little ones.

" What taste you do see displayed ! " Lottie remarked, sauntering to Kathie's vicinity. " Look at that woman's shawl with a yellow centre. Is n't it hideously ugly ? And that purple bonnet with red flowers ! Why did n't she put blue, by way of contrast ? "

The wearer of the purple bonnet glanced at the two girls with a flushed and rather indignant face, —

AT THE FAIR. Page 80.

a hard-featured countrywoman, neither young nor pretty.

" O don't," whispered Kathie. " She heard you."

" As if I cared ! Any person who outrages taste in that manner is a fit subject for criticism. How horridly that gored skirt hangs ! Home-made to the last thread. If I could n't have a dressmaker I would not have any new dresses."

Kathie was feeling quite distressed. She disliked to have Lottie to stand here and make remarks on every one who passed by.

" How do you make them 'ere things ? " inquired a coarse but fresh young voice at her side.

Lottie tittered, and put her handkerchief to her face.

" What ? " asked Kathie, in great confusion.

" These 'ere," pointing to some very pretty moss and lichen brackets.

" The moss is fastened to a piece of wood just the right shape, — like this " ; and she turned the bracket round.

" Pasted on ? "

" You could use paste or glue, — anything that adheres quickly."

6

" Adheres ? " — with a kind of wondering stare.

" Sticks ! " exclaimed Lottie, in a peculiar tone.

" I was n't talking to you," said the girl, rather gruffly.

Lottie tossed her head with a world of scorn, and moved a little lower down to speak to some stylish friends that she saw coming.

" Thinks she 's dre'dful fine ! " continued the girl. " You find them things in the woods. I have lots of 'em, but I never thought o' puttin' them up any- wheres. I 've some a good deal bigger 'n any you have here."

She was referring to the lichens now.

" They must be very fine," said Kathie.

" Some of 'em are pinky, and all streaked, in rows like this. Don't you s'pose I could put 'em up ? And I know Jim 'd make me some fine things to stick the moss on. He 's powerful handy with tools. Means to be a carpenter."

She was a nice, wholesome-looking girl of fifteen or thereabout. Kathie wished that she dared to cor- rect her words and sentences a little.

" You might make your parlor or your own room look very pretty with some of these adornments," she remarked, with quiet interest.

"The youngsters would soon smash 'em up in my room," she said, with rough good-nature; "but ma'am will let me fix up the parlor, I know. And if you 'd only tell me —" The girl wriggled around with painful hesitation.

"Well?" Kathie went on, encouragingly.

"About them 'ere frames that look like straw."

"They are straw."

"There, I was sure of it! Ain't they han'some! Do you know how to make 'em?"

"Yes."

"S'pose you would n't like to tell me?" — bashfully.

"Why, yes," answered Kathie, smiling. "First, you find some nice, long pieces of straw that are smooth and round, and, holding them together this way, — four or five or six, as wide as you want your frame, — sew them backwards and forwards with a fine needle and cotton. When you have made your four pieces cross them so, and fasten them through on the pictures at the corner. Then you tie a little bow over the sewing."

"Well, now, it is n't hard, after all! I mean to make some. What 's the price of that?"

" Fifty cents."

" I mean to have one of 'em. I 'll hunt up mother and come back." With that the girl dashed into the crowd.

" Profitable customer!" sneered Lottie.

Just then there was a rush to the table, and Kathie was kept very busy for ten minutes or so, while Lottie went over to Mrs. Wilder's table and began to " take off" Kathie's young woman, as she called her. It sounded very funny to the group of girls, exaggerated a little by Lottie's love of a good story.

Half an hour afterwards, when Kathie had almost forgotten, the girl came dragging her mother rather unwillingly up to the table.

" Here she is ! I 've made her come, though she said fust she would n't. But you was so real sweet to me that I could n't give it up."

Kathie recognized the identical purple bonnet and dull red roses, and she flushed a little at the woman's sharp scrutiny.

" You ain't the one that laughed awhile ago," she said, the features relaxing a little. " City gals may think themselves a heap finer than country folk, but I can see bad manners as quick as the next one."

" I was very sorry for it," exclaimed Kathie, in a low tone.

" Then my gal would n't give me any peace till I come back " — apparently much mollified. " Now, Sary Ann, where 's the picter you want ? "

" O, they 're all so *bew*-tiful ! " exclaimed the girl. " And I know I can make the frames after I go home. Look at this 'ere cross and this basket of flowers, and these roses ! O dear ! " — in despair.

" She 's so fond o' flowers, — is Sary Ann. She 's had the beautifullest garden this summer that you ever see. Well, Sary Ann ? I 'd take the basket of flowers."

" But the cross ! " exclaimed the girl, longingly.

They looked them over while Kathie went to wait upon another customer.

" I 've concluded to get 'em both for her," announced the woman. " Sary Ann 's a real good girl, and a powerful sight o' help to me. There 's six younger 'n she, and Jim older ; but boys can't do much about a house."

Kathie did up the pictures with a little sensation of triumph.

" O mother, look what a pretty baby's cap ! Would

n't it be sweet for Lily, and **you** promised to buy **her** one the **fust time** you went to town."

"She would have the baby called Lily," said the woman, **as if in** apology. "What 's the price **of** this ? "

"Two dollars and a half."

"O, that 's too dear."

"We have cheaper ones."

"But this is such a beauty," said **Sary Ann.**

"I crocheted it myself," Kathie returned, quietly.

"O mother, I 'd like to have something she 's done her **own very self!** Did you make the frames ? "

"No, my aunt did those, **but I** know how," — with a sweet smile.

After a good deal of talking they concluded **to** take the cap ; **then Sary Ann wanted** a pretty white apron for the "patron" of it, she declared.

"Nonsense ! " said her mother.

But Sary Ann **carried the** day, and afterward she found something else.

Altogether the bill amounted to seven dollars and sixty-four cents. Not so bad, after all. The woman paid it without a bit of grumbling.

"It's a good cause," she said. "I often think of the poor fellows out there," nodding her head; "and sence the Lord gives 'em strength and courage to go, we ought to do something besides prayin' for 'em. My old man he put up a lot of turkeys an' chickens, an' apples and onions, an' sez he, 'Though we ain't any children out there, we've neighbors and friends, and every chap among the lot deserves a Thanksgiving dinner.'"

Kathie forgot all about the red and purple, thinking of the red, white, and blue, and of the tender place in this woman's heart.

"I want to give you a little picture to frame," she said to "Sary Ann"; "it will help you to remember me, as well as the cause."

It was a pretty colored photograph of two children, — "The Reconciliation."

The girl was so delighted that the quick tears sprang to her eyes. "There's no fear of my forgetting you," she declared, warmly. "I've had a splendid time!"

Kathie opened her portmonnaie and dropped the quarter in the drawer. Her mother had taught her to be scrupulously honest about such matters, and she wanted the gift to be altogether hers.

It was getting quite dusky now.   Uncle Robert
had brought Mrs. Alston over in the pony-carriage,
and was to take Kathie back, " to smooth her ruf-
fled plumes," the child said; for the knot of girls
around Emma Lauriston had been discussing what
they would wear.

" There 'll be a great jam here to-night," said one.
" Everybody will turn out, and I want to look as
pretty as possible."

Kathie had begun to have some rather troublesome thoughts on the subject of dress.   The larger
girls at school talked considerably of the fashions.
She realized her own position much better than she
had a year ago, and knew that a certain style was
expected of her: She hated to be considered mean
or shabby, or, worst of all, deficient in taste ; yet how
much of it was right ?   Need it occupy all one's
time and one's desires ?

She felt very strongly inclined to make herself
" gorgeous " to-night, as Rob would have phrased it ;
yet the only ornament she indulged in was a little
cluster of flowers at her throat.

A jam it was, sure enough.   Everybody had to
look half a dozen ways at once.   The hum of the

laughing and talking almost drowned the music. By nine o'clock some of the tables began to wear a rather forlorn aspect, and two or three "shut up shop," having been entirely sold out.

Miss Weston's luck appeared less brilliant than that of many others.

"I wish you could take some one there who would buy ever so many things," Kathie said to Uncle Robert; "I am afraid she is feeling a good deal discouraged."

He smiled at the thoughtfulness, but made no immediate reply. Only Kathie noticed his standing there a considerable length of time.

When he came back to her he said, softly, "Kathie, will you not come and keep her table for a little while? I want to take her to the supper-room for some refreshments."

Kathie gave him a rather beseeching look.

"I'll be sure and not let her spend more than fifteen minutes. After that we will have a gay promenade."

Was it selfish not to want to stay here? Yet Kathie put on her most attractive smiles and actually sold several articles while Miss Weston was gone.

Then, hunting up Emma Lauriston, they set out on a tour, Uncle Robert said. They went to the Dutch kitchen, where Miss Jessie was one of the "young ladies" to-night; and very pretty she looked, though Uncle Robert insisted that she could not talk a word of Dutch. They had cream afterward, candy, nuts, and fruit, until it appeared to Kathie that she had eaten enough to last a week.

There had been a discussion at first about continuing the Fair on Thanksgiving day, but, as the articles were so nearly sold out, it was decided to have an auction. That made great fun indeed. By eleven o'clock the tables were emptied, and the refreshments reduced to a rather fragmentary state. The crowd, too, began to thin out.

Such a hunting for baskets and hampers and boxes of every description, such a hurrying and scurrying and confusion of voices, was seldom witnessed in quiet Brookside. In the crowd Kathie ran over Lottie.

"O dear!" the latter exclaimed, fretfully, "are n't you half tired to death, Kathie Alston? I 've ruined my dress too, — this lovely blue silk! I am sure I don't know what ma will say. Some one trod on it, as I was sitting down, and tore off the trimming, and that clumsy Harry Cox spilled lemonade on me. Children ought not to be allowed in such places, especially boys who do not know how to behave!" and she uttered this with a great deal of emphasis. "And I've lost one of my new kid gloves. They were such a lovely shade. There is nothing in Brookside like them!

"She ought to have known better than to dress in such state, as if she was going to a party," whispered Emma Lauriston. "I am cream and pie and cake-crumbs, and goodness only knows what, and devoutly thankful that I shall not have to go to school to-morrow. But it *has* been a success. Mrs. Wilder made one hundred and forty dollars at her table, — our table," with a laugh.

"And mamma has made nearly two hundred."

"I long to hear the aggregate."

"It will not be less than two thousand," exclaimed Uncle Robert, trying to open a path for the girls.

Kathie was very tired when she reached home, and with a good-night kiss ran off to her own room, where she fell asleep with a strange jumble of ideas in her head.

Two thousand three hundred and twenty dollars for the widows and orphans when all expenses were paid. Everybody felt very well satisfied, and, after a good Thanksgiving dinner, affairs at Brookside rolled on as calmly as before.

Except, perhaps, that there were more anxious hearts. General Sherman was sweeping on to the sea, and brave Sheridan was carrying consternation to the heart of the enemy by his daring raids. Grant was drawing nearer and nearer to Richmond, but there would be some pretty hard work at the last, every one thought.

Some days afterward Kathie finished a letter to Mr. Meredith, giving him a glowing account of their labors at home.

"If he could come back to keep Christmas with us!" Kathie said, longingly. "And dear Rob — and O, the hundreds more who are away from pleasant firesides!"

Uncle Robert decided to pay Rob a Christmas visit, and they concluded to pack a small box to send. He was so fond of "goodies" that Kathie tried her hand at some of the Fair recipes and had excellent success. A few new articles were needed for every-day use, but these comprised only a very small share.

"He will have quite a feast," Kathie said, delightedly. "And there is not much fear of Rob being like Harry in the story."

Uncle Robert would be back by Christmas. They had planned to have a tree again, but Kathie declared that she could not think of a single thing she needed. She was quite busy with various other little matters, however, that required strict seclusion in her own room.

How different it was from last year! She and Aunt Ruth talked it over, — the waiting, the disappointment, and the sacrifice that after all had ended so happily.

"It seemed as if everything must have happened then, and that there would be nothing left for this year," she said.

Uncle Robert brought most satisfactory accounts from his nephew. Rob was well, contented and happy, and growing tall in an astonishing manner. He sent oceans of love and thanks to everybody, and wished that he could come home and see them.

"And here is a letter for you," said Kathie, taking

it from the rack on his desk. "It is from Mr. Meredith. See if he is not going to surprise us. The ninety days will soon be ended."

Uncle Robert sat before the grate fire, sunning himself in the cheerful glow, but Kathie remarked that his face grew very grave.

"What is it?" she asked, anxiously. "He is not sick, or —"

"He is well. You may read this."

He folded down a little slip at the top and handed the letter to the child, who read: —

"Tell Kathie that I have seen General Mackenzie, her hero of last winter, and that he was delighted to have some tidings of her. And that during the last fortnight my ideas and sphere of duty seem to have enlarged. I think she will approve of my decision, — my brave little Captain who stood by her colors so nobly last winter, and preferred to minister to her suffering aunt rather than share the most tempting pleasures. So I shall give up my own comfort and idleness awhile longer, and stand by the dear country that needs every man in this last great struggle."

"Oh!" with a tender little cry. "He is not coming home!"

"No. He has resolved to stay and see the war through," was the grave reply.

Kathie looked into the glowing fire. It was very brave and noble in him for he did *not* like military life under the auspices in which he was seeing it.

"There is a little more," Uncle Robert said.

The "little more" brought the tears to her eyes. She stooped and laid her head on Uncle Robert's shoulder, nestling her face in the corner by his curly beard.

"He thinks — it will be — all right with him," she whispered, tremulously, a little sob quivering in her voice.

"Living or dying," returned Uncle Robert, solemnly. "My darling, I am very grateful for your share in the work. It seems to me that Mr. Meredith is capable of something really grand if he can once be roused to a sense of the responsibility and preciousness of life. There is so much for every one to do."

"But it does n't seem as if I did anything."

"No act is without some result, my dear child, when we think that it must all bear fruit, and that we shall see the result in the other country, whether it be brambles or leaves or fruit; and we cannot bear fruit except we abide in the Master."

It seemed to Kathie, child as she was, that she had a blessed glimpse of the light and the work, the interest and sympathy, the prayers and earnest endeavor, which were to go side by side with the Master's. A warm, vivifying glow sped through every pulse. Was this the love of God, — the grace which was promised to well-doing? She hardly dared believe, it was so solemnly sweet and comforting, — too good for her, she almost thought.

"You see, little one, that *He* puts work for us everywhere, that his love and presence is beside it always. We may wait a long while for the result, yet it is sure. And we need not be sparing of our seed; the heavenly storehouse is forever open to us. He is always more ready to give than we to receive."

"O Uncle Robert! I am so glad for — for Mr. Meredith. It seems as if I could n't take it all in at once!" and both of Kathie's arms were around his neck, her soft, rosy cheek, wet with tears, pressed against his.

"It is something to think of for all time, my darling."

"Uncle Robert," she said, after a long, thoughtful pause, in which she appeared to have glimpses of the life stretching out before her, and leading to the gate of the other country, "I used to wish that I could have — religion — myself, like mamma and Aunt Ruth — "

"My little Kathie, the 'kingdom of heaven' is within you. We have only to do *His* will, and we shall know of the doctrine. That is the grand secret of it all."

CHAPTER VI.

GIVING AND RECEIVING.

KATHIE had begged, instead of having anything grand herself, that she might be allowed to play Santa Claus. To be sure, there were gifts to the Morrisons, to Lucy and Annie Gardiner, and several of her olden schoolmates, but that was not quite it.

"I mean the highways and byways," she said to her mother; "some of the poor people who really have no Christmas."

They made out quite a list, — three or four widows with little children, some old women, and several homes in which there was sickness. Aunt Ruth fashioned some garments, — Kathie buying the material out of her Fortunatus's purse; two or three good warm shawls had been provided, and different packages of provisions, some positive luxuries. They stood in a great pile at the lower end of the hall, all ready for distribution.

" If you were not too tired —" Kathie said, after supper.

" I am not utterly worn out," and Uncle Robert smiled a little. " What is it ? "

" I wish you and I could go out with the gifts, instead of Mr. Morrison."

" Why not, to be sure ? " reading the wistful glance in the soft eyes.

" It would be so delightful. And as we are not to have our Christmas until to-morrow — "

" Bundle up then, for it is pretty sharp out. I will go and order the horses."

It was so easy to ride around and dispense benefits that Kathie almost wondered if there was any real merit in it.

" My little girl," Uncle Robert said, " you must not begin to think that there can be no religion without sacrifice. God gives us all things richly to enjoy, and it would be ungrateful if we did not accept the good, the joy."

All things. As they hurried softly on, the roads being covered with a light fall of snow, she drank in the beauty around her, — a glimmer of silvery moon-light flooding the open spaces, the shadowy thickets of evergreens, whose crisp clustering spines were stirred dreamily with the slow wind, making a dim and heavenly music, as if even now it might lead kings and shepherds to the place where the Christ Child had been born, the myriad of stars overhead in that blue, spacious vault, and the heaven above it all. And thinking of the distant plains of Judæa brought her to the plains nearer home, — the broad fields of Virginia dotted with its camps and tents, and bristling with forts. Thousands of men were there, keeping Christmas eve, and among them Mr. Meredith. How many beside him saw the star and came to worship the Saviour!

She felt the living Presence in the awe of this hush and beauty. Her child's soul was hovering on the point of girlhood, to open into something rare and precious, perhaps, having greater opportunities than many others. She was not so fearful or doubting as she had been an hour ago, for it seemed to her now that she had only to go forward.

They paused first at a little tumble-down cottage. There were seven people housed in it, — the old folks, Mrs. Maybin, whose husband had gone to the war, and four children. Mrs. Maybin went out washing and house-cleaning. Jane, the eldest daughter, thirteen, worked in the paper-mill.

Uncle Robert looked at the label by moonlight. " I 'll just put it down on the door-step and knock," he said. " You hold the ponies."

The knock made Kathie's own heart beat. Uncle Robert ran back to the carriage, which stood in the shade of a great black-walnut tree.

Kathie leaned over. Jane Maybin came to the door, lamp in hand, and looked around wonderingly. Then, spying the great bundle, she cried, loudly, " O mother, come here, quick ! "

The ponies wore no bells to-night, so they drove off noiselessly, a peculiar smile illuminating Kathie's face. If the Maybins thought their good fortune rained down from heaven, so much the better. The child was always a little shy of her good deeds, a rare and exquisite humility being one of her virtues. And though any little act of ingratitude touched her to the quick, she never went about seeking praise.

A dozen homes made glad by unexpected gifts, and three times that number of hearts. In several instances they had difficult work to escape detection, but that added to the fun and interest of it,

Kathie declared ; and she came home in a bright, beautiful glow, her cheeks glowing with a winter-rose tint, and her pretty mouth smiling in a more regal scarlet than the holly berries nodding their wise little heads above picture-frames.

Aunt Ruth kissed her quietly. It seemed as if she understood the steps in the new life which the child was taking, and knew by experience that silent ways were sometimes the most pleasant.

Of all Kathie's Christmas remembrances — and even Dr. Markham sent her a beautiful gift — there was one so unexpected and so touching that it brought the tears to her eyes. She was running through the hall just before church-time, when the door-bell rang ; the Alstons did not consider it necessary that Hannah should always be summoned from her duties to attend the call, so Kathie opened the door.

A stout, country-looking lad, just merging into awkward young-manhood, with a great shock of curly, chestnut-colored hair, and a very wide mouth, stood with a parcel in his hand.

" I want to see Miss Kathie Alston," he said, blushing as red as a peony.

"I am the person," she answered, simply.

He stared in surprise, opening his mouth until there seemed nothing but two rows of white, strong teeth.

"Miss — Kathie — Alston?" in a kind of astonished deliberation.

"Yes."

"I was to give this to you. She," nodding to some imaginary person, "told me to be sure to put it into your hands for fear. She thought you'd like it."

"Who is *she?*" and Kathie could not forbear smiling.

"She writ a letter so's you'd know. That's all she said, only to ask if you were well; but you look jest like — a picter."

The compliment was so honest and so involuntary that Kathie bowed, her bright face flushing.

He ran down the steps and sprang into a common country sleigh, driving off in a great hurry.

There was a letter attached to the parcel. She tore off the wrapping of the package first, however, and found that it had been done up with great care. Inside of all, the largest and most beautiful lichen she

had ever seen, — a perfect bracket in itself. The
rings of coloring were exquisite. The soft woody
browns, the bright sienna, the silvery drab and pink,
like the inside of a sea-shell. The vegetation was so
rank that it resembled the pile of velvet.

Like a flash a consciousness came over her, and
although she heard Aunt Ruth's voice, she could not
resist the desire to look at her letter.

A coarse, irregular hand, with several erasures and
blotted words, but the name at the bottom — Sarah
Ann Strong — made it all plain. The Sary Ann of
the Soldiers' Fair. Kathie's heart gave a great
bound.

"Come!" exclaimed Uncle Robert; "are you
ready?"

There was no time for explanations. She laid
the letter and parcel in her drawer in the great
bookcase, thrust her ungloved hands into her muff,
and ran out to Aunt Ruth, who stood on the step,
waiting to be assisted into the carriage.

"Was it some more Christmas?" asked Uncle
Robert, "or is it a secret?"

"It is no secret, but a very odd circumstance, and
has quite a story connected with it. I think I will

wait until we get home," she continued, slowly, re-membering how short the distance was to church, and that a break in the narrative would spoil it.

But she had very hard work to keep her mind from wandering during the service, she wondered so what Sarah had to say, and how she came to remember the simple talk about the brackets. And was Sarah having a bright Christmas?

Afterward she told her small audience, beginning with the unlucky remarks about the purple bonnet. Uncle Robert admired the lichen very much, and Aunt Ruth declared that she had never seen its equal.

Then came Sarah's letter. What pains and trouble and copying it had cost the poor girl Kathie would never know.

"To Miss Kathie Alston," it began. "I take my pen in hand to let you know that" — here were two or three words crossed out — "I want to send you a cristmas present. I haint forgot about the fair, and how good you was to me. I made some straw frames and they 're real hansum, and I put the picture you give me in one and it hangs up in the parlor, and I 've got some brackets, but Jim found this splendid one, and I want to send it to you for cristmas, for I don't think you have forgotten all about me. I 've been going to school a little this winter again, for Martha is big enough to help mother and i only stay home to wash. I always remember how beautiful you talked and my teacher says its grammar which I 'm studying, but I cant make head nor tail of it, but he told me never to say this ere, and I don't any more, but I never could be such a lady as you are. I spose you 've got beautiful long curls yet. I do love curls so and my hair 's straight as a stick. Mother says i must tell you if you ever come to Middleville to stop and see us, we live on the back road, Jotham Strong, and we 'll all be glad to see you. I hope you 'll like the bracket, and I wish you merry cristmas a thousand times. Jim went to town one day and found out who you was — he seen you the night of the fair too. Excuse all mistakes. I aint had much chance for schooling, but I 'm going to try now. I spose you are a lady and very rich, and don't have to do housework, but you 're real sweet and not stuck up, and so you 'll forgive the boldness of my writing this poor letter.

> "Yours respectfully,
> "SARAH ANN STRONG."

Kathie had been leaning her arm on Uncle Robert's knee as she read aloud.

"Not such a bad letter," he said. "I have known some quite stylish ladies 'who did n't have to do housework' to make worse mistakes than this girl, who evidently has had very little chance. And then country people do not always understand the advantages of education."

"I wanted to ask her that evening not to say 'this 'ere,' or 'that 'ere' so much, but I was afraid of wounding her feelings. I thought there was something nice about her, and her mother was very generous in buying. But to think that she should have remembered me all this while — "

"'A cup of cold water,'" repeated Aunt Ruth, softly.

"It was such a very little thing."

"One of the steps."

Yes. It was the little things, the steps, that filled the long, long path. A warm glow suffused Kathie's face. She was thinking far back, — an age ago it appeared, yet it was only two years, — that her mother had said the fairies were not all dead. If Puck and Peas-blossom and Cobweb and Titania no longer danced in cool, green hollows, to the music of lily bells, there were Faith and Love and Earnest Endeavor, and many another, to run to and fro with sweet messages and pleasant deeds.

"I am very glad and thankful that you were polite and entertaining," Uncle Robert remarked, presently. "We never know what a kind word or a little pains, rightly taken, may do. It is the grand secret of a useful life, — sowing the seed."

"I must answer her letter, and express my thanks. But O, is n't it funny that she thinks me such a great lady!"

"Suppose we should drive out to see her on some Saturday? Where is Middleville?"

"North of here," returned Aunt Ruth, "in a little sort of hollow between the mountains, about seven or eight miles, I should think."

"How delightful it would be!" exclaimed Kathie.

"We will try it some day. I am very fond of plain, social country people, whose manners may be unpolished, but whose lives are earnest and honest nevertheless. We cannot all be moss-roses, with a fine enclosing grace," said Uncle Robert.

Kathie read her letter over again to herself, feeling quite sure that Sarah had made some improvement since the evening of the Fair.

"Do you want to put the lichen up in your room?" asked Uncle Robert.

"Not particularly, — why?"

"It is such a rare and beautiful specimen that I feel inclined to confiscate it for the library."

"I will give it up with pleasure," answered Kathie, readily, "since it remains mine all the same."

The Alstons had a quiet Christmas dinner by themselves. Uncle Robert gave the last touches to the tree, and just at dusk the small people who had been invited began to flock thither. Kathie had not asked any of her new friends or the older girls. She possessed by nature that simple tact, so essential to fine and true womanhood, of observing the distinc- . tions of society without appearing to notice the different position of individuals.

Ethel Morrison came with the rest. She was beginning to feel quite at home in the great house, and yielded to Kathie's peculiar influence, which was becoming a kind of fascination, a power that might have proved a dangerous gift but for her exceeding truth and simplicity.

The tree was very brilliant and beautiful. If the gifts were not so expensive, they appeared to be just what every one wanted.   Kathie was delighted with the compliment to her discernment.

Charlie Darrell made his appearance quite late in the evening, with Dick Grayson.   The tapers were just burning their last.

"Farewell to thee, O Christmas tree!" sang Dick. "Was Santa Claus good to you, Miss Kathie?"

"Very generous indeed."

"But O, did n't you miss Rob?"

Kathie had to tell them about Uncle Robert's visit. "And then, you know, I was n't home last year" — in answer to their question.

"True.   There was a gay time here at Cedarwood. When Rob sets out, he is about as funny as any boy I know.   Don't you suppose he is just aching to be at home?"

"I expect to get off next year," said Dick, "to Yale.   But I shall be dreadfully homesick at first."

"So should I," responded Charlie; "but Rob is such a jolly, happy-go-lucky fellow."

"Has he been in any scrapes yet, Miss Kathie?"

"Not that I have heard," said Kathie, laughing.

A group around the piano were clamoring for Kathie to play.   She had promised them some carols.

Dick and Charlie joined. A happy time they had, singing everything they knew. Kathie had become a very fair musician already.

While the little ones were hunting up their wraps, Kathie lingered a moment beside Charlie.

" How is Miss Jessie to-night ? " she asked.

" Quite well." Then, looking into her eyes, " You have heard — "

" About Mr. Meredith ? yes."

" It is too bad, — is n't it ? And he has had a substitute in the war. I think he ought to have come back."

Kathie was silent. How much duty did a man or a woman owe to these great life questions ? And was there not something grander and finer in this last act of heroism than many people were capable of ? If she could have chosen for him, like Charlie, she would have desired his return ; but if every wife and every mother felt so about their soldiers ?

She kissed Ethel with a peculiar sympathy when she bade her good night. Mr. Morrison was well and satisfied with the new life, — liked it, indeed.

For the next fortnight it seemed to Kathie that nothing happened, — school life and home life, and she a little pendulum vibrating between the two, waiting for some hour to strike.

She answered Sarah's letter, and promised that she and her uncle would drive up when there came a pleasant Saturday with the roads in comfortable order.

There had been quite an accession to the school on the first of January. Mrs. Wilder had twenty-one pupils now. Mr. Lawrence came in to give them lessons in music, French, and penmanship. Kathie felt quite small, there were so many young ladies.

Several new families had moved into Brookside the preceding summer, and the Alstons' acquaintance had slowly widened among the better class. Kathie remembered how grand she had once considered Miss Jessie, and now she was really beyond that herself.

At twelve the girls had fifteen minutes' intermission. Sometimes they took a little run through the long covered walk, but oftener gathered around the stove or visited at one another's desks. There was always a vein of school-girlish gossip on dress, or amusements, or parties, or perhaps the books they were reading. This generally took in the circle just above Kathie, yet she used occasionally to listen, and it always brought a thought of Ada to her mind.

She sat puzzling over some French verbs one rainy day, while Emma brought out her cathedral that she was doing in India-ink. The talk from the group before them floated to their hearing. It was styles and trimming, velvet and laces that were "real," and gloves with two buttons.

Emma glanced up with an odd smile. Kathie, seeing it, smiled too.

"Let us take a turn in the walk," Emma said.

She was so much taller that she put her arm around Kathie with an odd, elder-sisterly feeling.

"They seem never to get tired of it," she began. "I wonder if there is n't something better to this life than the clothes one wears?"

"Yes," Kathie answered, in a slow, clear tone, though she shrank a little from giving her opinion. She had a shy desire to escape these small responsibilities, yet the consciousness of "bearing witness" always brought her back.

"What is it?"

The blunt question startled her, and a faint color stole into her face.

8

"I watch you sometimes when I suppose you are not dreaming of it. We have been sitting here together for three months, we were at the Fair, — and there is something different about you from what I find in most girls. I wonder if it is your taste or your nature."

"We are none of us' alike," said Kathie, with a peculiar half-smile.

"It is not that specific difference which we all have. You appear to be thinking of others, you never answer crossly, you often give up your own ease and comfort, and there is a little light in your eyes as if something out of your soul was shining through them. And all this talk about dressing and what one is going to do by and by never touches you at all. I suppose you could have everything you want! Lottie Thorne says your uncle idolizes you, and — he is rich, I know."

"I have all that is necessary, and many luxuries," Kathie answered, slowly.

"But what makes you — what keeps you in such a heaven of content? O, I can't explain what I mean! I wonder if you have religion, Kathie Alston."

Do her best, Kathie could not keep the tears out of her eyes. What was there to cry about? But somehow she felt so strange and shy, and full of tender pain.

"I think we ought all to try," she answered, with a sweet seriousness in her voice. "Even if we cannot take but one step — "

"I wish I knew *what* it was!"

Kathie's heart was in her throat. She only understood part of the steps herself. How could she direct another? So they took two or three turns in silence, then the bell rang.

"There! I had so much to say, and maybe I shall never feel in the mood again. About dress, too. Some of it troubles me sadly."

She stooped suddenly and kissed Kathie on the forehead, gave her hand a sudden, earnest pressure, and then was her olden grave self.

And Kathie wondered a little if she had not shirked a duty! It seemed now as if it would be very easy to say, "I have enlisted in that greater army of the Lord, and will do what service I can." Why had it been so hard a moment ago? Had she been challenged at the outpost and found without a countersign?

CHAPTER VII.

A VISIT.

"Do you think we could go to Middleville to-day?" Kathie asked, one bright Saturday morning.

It was a sharp, keen winter's day, but the roads had been worn tolerably smooth with the sleighing, and it was by far too cold for alternate freezing and thawing; but the sky was of a clear, steely blue, and the sun as brilliant as a midwinter's sun could be.

"If you did not mind the cold. What is your opinion, Dora?" — turning to Mrs. Alston.

"I suppose you could stand it if you were wrapped up good and warm."

"Would you take the buggy?" asked Aunt Ruth.

"O yes!" answered Kathie, eagerly; "I cannot bear to be shut up in a close prison, as if I was being taken off somewhere for my misdeeds."

"It will be a good deal colder."

Uncle Robert laughed as he met Kathie's mirthful eyes.

"I shall not freeze, auntie. I like the sensation of this strong, fresh wind blowing square into my face; it takes the cobwebs out of my brains."

So the ponies had orders, and pricked up their ears as if they were rather interested in trying the bracing wind as well.

Kathie bundled herself up quite to mamma's liking. She slipped a little parcel under the seat, — two books that she had read time and again, and which she fancied might interest Sarah, and a few other little matters, the giving of which depended upon circumstances.

They said good by, and were off. "Up in the mountains" was always spoken of rather sneeringly by the Brookside community. They really were not mountains, but a succession of rough, rocky hills, where the vegetation was neither lovely nor abundant. Several different species of cedar, scrubby oaks, and stunted hemlocks, were the principal variety, with a matted growth of underbrush; and as there were many finer "woods" around Brookside, these were seldom haunted by pleasure-lovers or wonder-seekers.

The dwellers therein were of the oldest-fashioned

kind.   You could always tell them when they came
to shop at Brookside by their queer bonnets and out-
of-date garments, as well as by the wonderful contrast
of colors.   But the small settlements enjoyed their
own manner of living and their own social pleasures
as thoroughly as their more refined neighbors.

For quite a stretch the road was level and good,
then the ascent began, the houses were wider apart,
and with an air of indifference as to paint and repairs,
while fences seemed to be vainly trying to hold each
other up.

The ponies were fresh and frisky, and did not
mind the tug.   Kathie was silent for the most part,
her brain in a kind of floating confusion, not at all
unpleasant, but rather restful.

"Now, which is the back road, I wonder?" said
Uncle Robert, slowly, checking the horses a trifle.

Both roads were exceedingly dreary-looking, but
they decided to take the one farther north, and before they had gone a quarter of a mile they met a
team, driven by a young lad.

"Is this Middleville?" asked Uncle Robert.

"Yes."

"Which is the back road?"

" Keep straight along.   You 're right."

" Where does Mr. Jotham Strong live ? "

" Over there in that yaller house," the boy answered, nodding his head.

The place began to take on quite a village look.
There was a brown, weather-beaten meeting-house, a
small country store, and houses scattered around at
intervals.   Some were quite tidy-looking, but the
most had a kind of dilapidated air.

Mr. Strong's was large and roomy on the ground-
floor, as numerous additions had been made on three
sides of the building.   There was a door-yard in
front, where in summer they must have an abundance of roses, and two wide flower-beds down the
path.   Such signs went to Kathie's heart at once.

Uncle Robert sprang out and knocked at the door.
The hard-featured face that Kathie remembered so
well in connection with the purple bonnet peered
through the kitchen window.

The child would have laughed at the commotion
inside, if she could have seen it, — how Sary Ann
dragged the floating ends of her hair into a knot,
caught up a towel and wiped her face, making it
redder than before, jerked down her sleeves, which,

having neither hooks nor buttons, hung round her wrists.

She stared as she opened the door to a strange man, but glanced past him to the carriage.

"I have brought Miss Kathie Alston up to see you," Mr. Conover announced, in his warm, cheerful voice, for he recognized Sarah from Kathie's graphic description.

"O my! and I 'm all in a heap; but I 'm so glad!" and she ran out to the wagon, but stopped at the gate with a sudden sensation of bashfulness, and a wonder if she ought not to have said something more to the gentleman.

"How do you do, Sarah?" Kathie's voice was like the softest of silver bells pealing on the frosty air.

"O, I 'm so glad! I did n't hardly believe you 'd come. I looked last Sat'day. Your letter was so nice. I 'm glad you liked the lichen. Jim and me hunted over hundreds of 'em, and found the very biggest. Do get out and come in the house; you must be perished! Is that the uncle you wrote about in your letter?"

"Yes." Uncle Robert had come down the path by this time. "My uncle, Mr. Conover," Kathie said, gracefully, "and Miss Sarah Strong."

Sarah made a dash at her hair again as if she was afraid of its tumbling down, and courtesied to Uncle Robert so in the style of a country school-girl that he smiled inwardly. " O, coax her to get out ! " she exclaimed, appealingly. " I 've got a fire all ready to light in the best room, and I want you to see my pictures," — with a very long emphasis on the last syllable. " Mother 'xpects you to stay to dinner, and my Sat'day's work is 'most done. Come in, — do."

By this time Mrs. Strong had made herself tidy and appeared at the hall door.

" Come in," she exclaimed, cordially, — " come in. Sary Ann, show the gentleman how to drive right down to the barn. Jim 's there thrashin', and he 'll see to the hosses ! "

Kathie was handed out. Sarah turned the horses to face the path to the barn.

" Down there," she said. " Steve, come here ! "

Steve, thirteen or thereabout, sheepishly obeyed, and took the rest of his sister's order in silence.

" Don't you go," said Mrs. Strong to Mr. Conover. " There 's boys enough to the barn, and they know all about hosses. Come in an' get warm. You must be about froze ! I 'm right glad to see you, child."

Kathie introduced Uncle Robert again. **They were** marshalled into a large, uncarpeted kitchen, full of youngsters, with a great red-hot stove in their midst.

"Get out of the way, childern! Sary Ann, run light the fire in the parlor while they 're gettin' warm."

"It is not worth while to take that trouble," returned Uncle Robert. "We came up for a call, but judged it best to take the pleasantest part of such a cold day. So do not let us interfere with your usual arrangements."

"You ain't a goin' to stir a step until after dinner. Sary 'll be awful disapp'inted. We 've plenty of everything, and you won't put us out a bit. We 've been looking for you, like, ever sence Sary Ann had her letter. Take off your things, child! Ain't your feet half froze?"

"O no."

There was no resisting, however. Mrs. Strong talked and worked, tumbled over the children, picked them up and set them on chairs, bidding them keep out of the way, insisted that Kathie should sit beside the roasting stove, and presently Sarah returned. She had brushed her hair into a more respectable shape, and tied a most unnecessary scarlet ribbon in it, seeing that the hair was of a sandy reddish color.

But her clean calico dress certainly did improve her. Yet as she entered the room she was seized with a fit of awkward bashfulness.

"I believe I will go out and look at the ponies," remarked Mr. Conover.

"Mind they 're put out. You 're not going to stir a step till you 've had your dinner. Marthy, you peel them taters; quick now." This to a rather pretty girl of ten, who had been writing with a pin on the steamed window-pane.

"Come in the other room," said Sarah to Kathie.

The child followed. It was not very warm yet, but there was a great crackling, blazing fire upon the hearth, which was a delightful picture in itself.

Sarah stood and viewed her guest wonderingly. The long golden curls, the clear, fine complexion, the neat-fitting dress, the small white hands, and the dainty kid boots, were all marvels to her.

"You 're very rich," she said, presently, in a peculiar manner, as if she could almost find it in her heart to envy Kathie and grow discontented with herself. Kathie's fine sense and tact detected it.

She stretched out her hand and took Sarah's, — a little rough, but soft and plump. "My uncle is," she answered; "he is very good to us children. My father died when I was a tiny little girl."

"Did he?" Sarah knelt down, and began to wind the silken curls over her finger. "But you are so — so different. You don't have to work, — do you?"

"A little," and Kathie smiled.

"What! a lady like you? Don't you keep servants? For Jim said the place was like a palace!"

"We keep one servant only, and a gardener. Mamma thinks it right that every one should learn to be useful."

"But if I was rich I would n't do a thing! I actually would n't."

"I am afraid you would soon get tired of idleness."

"O, I 'd have books, and read, and paint pictures, and a pianny —"

"Piano," corrected Kathie, gravely, as if she had been a teacher with her class.

Sarah turned scarlet, then gave a little embarrassed laugh. "I never can get the words all right. They do plague me so; but I have n't been to school for two years. Mother wanted me home, for Martha was so little. That 's why I 'd like to be a lady, and know just what was right to do and say. I thought you was so elegant that night ! "

" There are a great many 'ladies,' as you call them, much poorer than you ; and some rich people who are coarse and ignorant."

"There ain't only two or three men in Middleville any richer than father. He owns sights of land and timber, but he thinks that if you can read and write and cipher a little it is enough. I don't suppose I could ever be as nice as you are, though," — with a sadness in her tone and a longing in her eyes.

" In what respect ? " Kathie smiled encouragingly.

" Well — to talk as you do. I thought that night at the Fair that it was just like a story-book or music. I know I 'm always makin' mistakes."

" Then you must try to be careful. Does not your teacher correct you ? "

" Well, I am learning a little ; but it seems to be such hard work. How did you do it ? "

" I have always been sent to school, and then my mother has taken a good deal of pains with me. It seems unfortunate that people should fall into such careless habits of pronouncing, and oftentimes of spelling."

"Was my letter all right?" Sarah asked, with quick apprehension. "I tried so hard, and wrote it over ever so many times."

"I let my uncle read it, and he said he had seen letters from older women that would hardly bear comparison. There were very few mistakes in it."

Kathie's honesty impelled her to say this, though under some circumstances she would have uttered no comment.

"Tell me what they were. I think I could do better now."

"Do you really wish me to?"

"Yes, I do," with a good deal of rising color.

"Your pronoun I, when you speak of yourself, must always be a capital, — never a small i, and dotted."

"But how can you tell?"

"It is a personal pronoun, and is never used in any other way. A single I must always be a capital."

"Always! I'll be sure to remember that," Sarah answered, with great earnestness; "and what else?"

"Christmas was n't quite right. That begins with a capital, because it is a proper name, and the first syllable is spelled just like Christ."

" Is it ?   Why, I never thought ! and I 've seen it
so many times too. What other mistakes were there ? "

" I really cannot remember," said Kathie, laughing ; and she spoke the truth. " The lichen was so
lovely, Uncle Robert put it up in the library. Where
do you find such beautiful specimens ? "

" Over in the swamp, about a mile south of here.
There are so many pretty things. Do you know
Indian pipe ? "

" Yes !" exclaimed Kathie, with a touch of enthusiasm.

" Is n't it lovely ? — just as if it was cut out of white
wax. I like to go rambling round to find all manner
of odd things ; but I never thought of putting them
up anywhere, or making frames. O, come see mine ! "

Both girls rose, and Kathie really took her first
survey of the parlor. There was a dull-colored in-
grain carpet on the floor, the flowers of which ran all
over it ; a square, stiff-backed sofa, studded with brass
nails ; some rush-bottomed chairs, two old family
portraits, and a pair of high brass candlesticks on
the mantelpiece.

But above this Sarah had hung her two pictures,
and put up the lichen brackets.

"I could n't make my frame as pretty as yours," she said; "and I broke ever so many straws."

"But you succeeded very well, I think."

"And I made this. I took the picture out of a book."

It was a moss frame, very neatly manufactured, but the picture was a rather coarsely colored fashion-plate.

"I do love pictures so! I wish I had a whole houseful! And if I could only make 'em myself, — them, I mean," coloring, and correcting her speech.

"I have brought you two more — O, they were left in the wagon ! — and some books."

Sarah's eyes sparkled. "Would you mind running out? The boys have some rabbits down to the barn, and there 's a great swing, — O, and loads of nuts! Do you ever go chestnutting?"

"I have been, but there are not a great many trees around Brookside."

"Here 's a shawl; just wrap yourself head and ears in it. We 're going down to the barn, mother."

They found Uncle Robert entertaining Jim and Steve, the latter of whom sat in wide-eyed astonishment; but the entrance of the girls broke up the conclave.

Sarah took Kathie all round, showed her White-
foot and Jenny, both of whom whinnied gratefully.
Then there was the beautiful little Durham heifer
that Jim was raising, hens of every variety, the
rabbits, the loft strewn with corn, nuts, and strings,
and packages of seeds.

Then Kathie must swing. Steve pushed her until
the dainty kid boots touched the beam, and she expe-
rienced the sensation of standing upon her head.

In the midst of this a shrill blast from a horn
reached their ears. Kathie started.

"That's for dinner. Father's gone to mill to-day
with Mr. Ketcham, and he won't be home."

The three younger ones took the lead, while Uncle
Robert and Jim lingered behind, discussing ways and
means of making money at farming.

Such a table full of youngsters looked strange
to Kathie's eyes. On the whole they behaved very
well, a little awed, perhaps, by the presence of
strangers. Sarah paused now and then to watch
Kathie, whose quiet manners were "so like a lady."
She made no clatter with her knife and fork, did not
undertake to talk with her mouth full, and said
"Thank you" to everything that was handed to her.

9

"I never can be like that!" she thought with a despairing sigh, and yet unconsciously her manners took tone from this unobtrusive example.

Uncle Robert and Kathie made themselves at ease with truest politeness. Mrs. Strong talked over the Fair, and how much she enjoyed it, and told Kathie that the children were delighted with their gifts. Then followed some conversation on the war. The Strongs were very patriotic, to say the least. Sarah was excused from helping to wash the dishes, so she and Kathie went to the parlor again, and the package was opened.

A very pretty story-book, one of Kathie's favorites, and a copy of Longfellow's Evangeline, illustrated. She had also brought two colored photographs, — the sad-eyed Evangeline, and the "Children," companion pictures.

"I don't know whether you like poetry or not, but it always seems to me that it is pleasant to know the story of anything that interests you."

"I like — some verses —" Sarah returned, rather hesitatingly, "and the book is beautiful. But — I can't say anything at all —"

The tears were so near to her voice that it rendered her almost ungracious.

"You will enjoy them better by and by," Kathie went on, softly. "Some day you may be able to make pretty frames for the pictures. And I brought you a set of crochet-needles. Can you crochet?"

"Only to make a chain. I can do that with my fingers. I wish I did know how. And if I could ever knit a cap like the baby's!"

"We will sit down here and talk, and I can show you one or two patterns of edgings that are simple and pretty."

"How good you are!"

Sarah was no dullard, after all. Though her fingers appeared rather clumsy at first, she soon managed to conquer the intricate loops, turnings, and stitches.

"Why, I would n't have believed it!" — in great joy. "I 've done a whole scallop by myself."

Kathie laughed in answer.

"Now, if you 'll only tell me something more about grammar, and putting the right word in — the place where it belongs. You see all the big girls at school know so much more than I do —"

Kathie understood. She explained several matters that had been great mountains to her in the beginning.

Now and then a bright light illumined the clear hazel eye, and a pleased smile played around the lips. "How good you are to take so much trouble!" she exclaimed, gratefully.

By and by Mrs. Strong came in to have a little visit with their guests. Sarah displayed the books and pictures, and the three inches of rather soiled crocheted edging.

"Sary Ann's a curis girl," explained her mother; "she has a great notion of larnin', and all that, but her father has n't much faith in it. He thinks gals and wimmen were a good deal better when they did n't know so much; and then you begin to want — everything. There's so much dressin' and foolin' goin' on nowadays."

"It is rather the lack of education, I should imagine. True knowledge expands one's soul as well as one's mind," said Uncle Robert.

"Well, mebbe, if it's the right sort; but this gettin' their heads so full of dress — "

"Which is a sign that something better should be in them," was the pleasant response.

"And then they 're ashamed of their homes, and their parents as slaved to bring them up, and make fun of everything that is n't right according to their thinking. I 've seen it more 'n once."

Kathie blushed, remembering Lottie Thorne's criticism. Mrs. Strong certainly did look prettier in this clean calico gown and white collar than in her purple bonnet with red roses.

"Yes," he answered; "it does happen, I know. But it seems to me that any daughter or sister who acquired with her other knowledge true views of her duty towards God and those around her could hardly fail to be benefited by an enlargement of her narrow sphere of thought. Our first duty is at home, but we do not stop there."

"Few people think of duties of any kind nowadays."

"Does not God leave a little to us? We who know them ought to make them attractive to others."

"It 's so much easier to be bad; and I often wonder at it," whispered Sarah, through Kathie's shimmering curls. "But if some one would make all that is right and good attractive, as your uncle says— I wish I could live with you awhile. I don't believe you ever have anything to worry you!"

"Yes, I do," answered Kathie; "I have to try pretty hard sometimes."

Sarah studied her in surprise. "But if I were to try I never could be half so good."

"Will you try?" Kathie uttered it with unconscious earnestness, and the light that so often shone about her came out in her face.

But Uncle Robert, looking at his watch, declared that it was time for them to go. Mrs. Strong was so sorry not to have "Father" see them, and begged them to come again.

"It 's been such a beautiful visit," exclaimed Sarah, with a tremble in her voice. "I 'll try to remember everything you have told me!"

Steve brought a bag of nuts to put in the wagon, and Jim shook hands rather sadly with Uncle Robert.

"He is one of the right kind"; and with that he went back to the barn, whistling thoughtfully.

CHAPTER VIII.

COMFORT IN NEED.

"Well, Kathie, was the visit a success?"

They had ridden a long way before Uncle Robert asked this question. He had been remarking the changes that passed over Kathie's face like light drifts of summer clouds.

"I am very glad that we went."

"What perplexes you then, Kitty?"

"A good many things, Uncle Robert. Some grave questions that I cannot understand," in a half-hesitating way.

"Can I help you?" The tone was gravely sweet.

"You always do," — smiling. "Something Mrs. Strong said troubled me. Sarah *is* ambitious, she has a desire for education, and a longing for refinement," — with deliberation in her slow tones. "But what if — she *should* be ashamed of her home, after all? It is not so very attractive, — pretty, I mean. Why, the only lovely thing in that great parlor was the bright blazing fire."

"If Sarah takes hold of the right end of life, she will try to make her home more pleasant for the others as well as herself."

"But, Uncle Robert, it is so hard to see when you are right in the midst of a thing, — a sort of muddle. A person standing on the outside would be likely to discover the best paths. And I thought — what if I should be the means of making her discontented instead of happy."

"So you are not quite convinced that it is wisest to sow beside all waters ?" — with his peculiar smile.

"If I was certain I had the right seed."

"The seed is all alike, — love, faith, patience. Yes, I can catch your meaning," — as the little face grew very sober. "You do not want to rouse her to a sense of and love for beauty to which she can never attain."

"That is it."

"I do not imagine you need begin to feel anxious immediately. Her crude attempts at beautifying will be very good exercise for her awakening brain, and she has so much of the practical to learn that she will be less likely to run into vanity, at least no more than one would naturally expect. If you choose, Kathie, you might help her in a very good work."

" I do choose."

" When you find that **you** have too much on your small hands, **you** must pass the heaviest over to **me**. Remember that **I** shall always stand ready. And doing these bits of girl-work for girls will make the woman-work plainer **by** and by. It is taking up the little opportunities as they come, not waiting for a great deed to be shaped to your hand presently."

"I think **I** must always **do** little deeds. They seem so much safer **to me than** the large ones."

"I heard Sarah ask **if she** might write **to** you; what did you answer?"

"**I** said that I should be glad **to hear.** And **I** shall want to know how she likes **her books.** You do not think mamma would object?"

" O no. **It is the** best and wisest act that you could **do for her.** There was something so sweet and grateful in her sending you the lichen that I **have** a good deal of faith in her capabilities. **It will be** good ground **in** which to sow seed. Sarah's whole life may be the better for **the** chance friendship."

" But **if she** should become refined and — "

" That is looking to **the** flavor of **the** fruit, my dear. **God means** that we shall not see it any faster than it **can** grow."

She smiled, satisfied.

The air was very keen indeed now. A bitterly cold night it would be. The tender heart went out to the thousands on "tented field," and prayed for peace, that they might return to warm, pleasant firesides.

Aunt Ruth ran down stairs as she saw them coming.

"Let Freddy take the horses," she said. "A telegram has come for you, and it may be important."

Freddy was elated with the permission. He was indulged now and then with short drives, but, being rather anxious to display his skill, he was sometimes quite venturesome.

Kathie drew a long, anxious breath. As was natural, her first thought was for Rob.

An expression serious almost to pain crossed Uncle Robert's face.

"Sad tidings for the close of our happy day," he said. "I am summoned to Alexandria immediately. Mr. Meredith —" Then he handed the slip of paper to Kathie.

Mr. Meredith had been severely wounded, and sent to the hospital at Alexandria, whether fatally or not the message did not state.

"The express train goes through at six," Uncle Robert said, "and in this case there is no time to be lost."

They all felt that when Mr. Meredith sent, the summons must be urgent indeed. Mr. Conover had more than an hour to make the few preparations he would require. But there were two or three letters to answer, so he went to the library, while Mrs. Alston hurried the tea.

Kathie stood by the window in a mood of peculiar silence. Somehow, though she had known the danger all along, with the confidence of love she could hardly believe that any evil would betide her soldiers. Numbers of men had served their three years without any serious mishap, and it seemed as if God would watch over these two among the many thousands.

"Aunt Ruth, do you suppose—"

"My darling, we can suppose nothing, only hope for the best."

"But it is so terrible to think of him—in any great peril."

So gay and laughing always, so full of vivacity with all his gentlemanly indolence, so strong and buoyant ! In fancy she saw him stretched upon a hospital pallet, very white, like Aunt Ruth, last winter, or perhaps having undergone some fearful operation.

And then there came to Kathie a remembrance of the last drive together, of the few lines in the letter. It was so precious to know that, living or dying, all was well with him. Kathie clung to that comfort with all her fond, trembling heart. Was it God's love and grace that brought human souls so near together and made them one great family ?

"I have one request to make," exclaimed Uncle Robert, entering the room ; "if you should see any of the Darrells do not mention this circumstance, unless they may have heard. I will telegraph home as soon as I reach the hospital, and write at my earliest convenience. Kathie, will you run over to the Lodge and ask Mr. Morrison to drive me to the station by six ? "

Kathie wrapped up head and ears in a blanket-shawl, and ran down the drive. When she came back supper was ready and Uncle Robert's portmanteau packed.

They bade him a tender good-by, and Kathie whispered a fond and precious message.

Afterward they went to Aunt Ruth's sitting-room. Kathie felt rather drowsy and indolent with her ride through the keen air, and took possession of Aunt Ruth's lounge; for she was in no mood to read or sew, or even to take up her fancy crocheting.

"Did you have a nice visit?" asked her mother, at length.

That roused Kathie. "It was very peculiar, mamma, and I enjoyed it a good deal. I like Sarah, although she is not —"

"Not much cultivated, I suppose," said Aunt Ruth.

"Mamma, why did not we, when we were very poor, grow careless? I don't know as I can explain just what I mean." Kathie raised her face, perplexed and rosy.

"I think I understand. It is not the result of a few years, or even of poverty, but the lack of culture. Often a whole village or settlement, where there is no particular ambition for education, will fall into careless and rough habits of action and speech. Every one does the same, and it is hardly remarked."

"But I suppose there has always been a school at

Middleville, — and it is so near Brookside and other towns."

"Many of these old country settlers are very sensitive. They think their way as good as any one's, and, if a few families are particularly refined, accuse them of holding themselves in high esteem, and being above their neighbors. It often proves difficult to overcome old habits of pronunciation and the manners and customs to which one has always been used. It was different in our case. Aunt Ruth and I were brought up in a city, and had the best advantages. I was not very likely to forget what I had learned as a girl."

It *did* make some difference, then, whether a person was rich or poor ; and if one could not help his or her position —

"Mamma, was n't it very hard to lose your fortune ?"

"Yes, dear," Mrs. Alston answered, simply.

"But we might have been poorer still. There are all the Maybins — and the Allens — and we had a very comfortable home."

"Yes. We owned our cottage, and had an income of just seventy dollars a year. It was a great deal better than nothing, though many a stitch had to be taken to provide for the rest of our needs."

Kathie remembered,—staying in the house to sew long simple seams for mamma, doing errands, washing dishes, sweeping rooms, and wearing dresses that were faded, shoes a little shabby, and never having more than a few pennies to spend. How great the change was! And it did not end with personal comforts merely. Nearly all the rich people in the neighborhood came to visit them. Every one nodded to her as she drove out in her pony-carriage. Yet, if she lost her fortune, would they let her drop out of sight and out of mind? Ah, how very cruel it would be!

"It is a very delightful thing to have an abundance," Mrs. Alston went on, as if she held the key to her daughter's thoughts. "Not that it ever makes a person better, socially or morally, though the world, society, generally gives the precedence to money. It affords you leisure for cultivation; it frees you from a great many harassing cares, though it may bring others in their stead, for no life is exempt. And it certainly does add many new duties."

"It is right to have the cultivation, the pretty

houses, the beautiful furniture and pictures and —
dresses ? "

Kathie asked **her** question with a sort of hurried
abruptness, as if a definite answer was of the utmost
importance to her, as if, indeed, she longed for a fuller
understanding of the subject.

" Yes," answered **her** mother, slowly. " All these
things were given to us to enjoy, to use, yet not
abuse. But **when we seek** them selfishly, when we
think of nothing beyond **our own** personal needs, and
of ministering to our **vanity and** self-love, they do
become a great snare and temptation."

" If one could tell just where the dividing line
ought to be," Kathie said, shyly.

" It is quite easily found if one searches in earnest :
to think of others rather than of one's self; to give
as well as to receive, not merely money or clothes,
but sympathy, love, tender thoughts, little acts of
pleasure; to minister to the poor in spirit as well as
the poor in purse."

" And that brings me back to Sarah, mamma.
Her father may be as rich as — we are," rather hesitatingly. " At all events Mrs. Strong spent a good
deal at our table at the Fair, and never seemed to

mind it a bit. But their house has such a barren look. They have very few books or pictures or pretty articles of any kind, yet I do believe Sarah would be very fond of them. She has not been to school for nearly two years, so she has had very little chance to improve. Her father is afraid that if she should learn a great deal she will be ashamed of her home, and all that. I do not see how she could like it very much, because there is so little in it to please."

"Some old-fashioned people seem to be afraid of education, but I believe it is from a lack of true appreciation of it. Whether rightly or not, civilization has made our wants extend beyond the mere necessities of life. We need some food for the soul as well as for the body."

"But if education should make Sarah discontented and unhappy?"

"We cannot always see what the result will be, but we are exhorted to work, nevertheless."

"She asked me to write to her again, mamma. You do not think it will be—" Kathie could hardly get hold of the right word to use.

"Injudicious, I suppose you mean? No, I do not. You may learn something as well."

Kathie was glad that her mother looked upon it in that light, and yet she smiled a little to herself, not exactly discerning her own lesson in the matter.

"Our Saviour said, 'Freely ye have received, freely give'; and, my little girl, it seems to me that we have received very generously. When I was prosperous before, I am afraid that I did not think much of the needs of those around me; but in my poverty I saw so often where a little would have been of great assistance to me. I feel now as if God had placed a great treasure in my hands to be accounted for to the uttermost farthing at the last day. It will be good then to have other lips speak for us."

Kathie understood. "Yes, it will, mamma." Then she lapsed into silence. How all these things crowded upon one as the years went by! Fourteen now; in three years she would be quite a young lady. Looking at it caused her to shrink back to the cloisters of girlhood.

Afterward her heart wandered out with Uncle Robert on his lonesome night-journey, and to the other face pictured still and white before her. All she could do in this case was to pray.

They went to church on Sunday, and saw Miss

Jessie, bright and smiling as usual. Then she did not know ! It actually startled Kathie a little.

" Where is your uncle ? " Charlie asked, as they were standing together.

" He was called away upon some business," Mrs. Alston answered for Kathie.

The telegram came on Monday. " Arrived safely," it said. " No .change in Mr. Meredith. Look for a letter to-morrow."

So they could still tell nothing about him. Kathie had grown so very anxious that it appeared as if she could not wait. The day was a little cloudy, and she made that an excuse for not driving out. Even her music failed to interest. She just wanted to sit and wonder, never coming to any definite conclusion.

The Tuesday letter was long, written at intervals, and contained the whole story. Mr. Meredith was out with a scouting-party early in the week before, when they were surprised by the enemy and made a desperate resistance. But for his coolness and bravery none of them would have escaped. Two or three were killed and several wounded, — he very seriously indeed ; and he had been sent immediately to Alexandria. The journey had doubtless aggravated

the injury. He was in a high fever now; and though
he had recognized Mr. Conover at first, he soon lapsed
into forgetfulness again.   Mr. George Meredith had
been on, and was unable to remain; but Uncle Robert
had decided that this was his post of duty for the present.   He had also written to Miss Jessie, he said.

"We must give him up willingly, therefore," Mrs.
Alston remarked.

Yes; Kathie least of all felt inclined to grudge
another the cheerful, comforting presence.

"But it is terrible!" she said; "it did not seem to
me as if Mr. Meredith *could* die."

"He may not. If they can succeed in keeping the
fever under control there will be hope.   The wound
itself is quite manageable, Uncle Robert believes."

But by the end of the week Miss Jessie and her
father had been summoned.   There was very little if
any hope.

One of Ada's occasional letters reached Kathie
about this time. "Is n't it dreadful?" she wrote.
"Mamma says that she can hardly forgive Uncle
Edward for going in the first place, when there really
was no need, and he was crazy to enlist afterward;
and it puts everything out so! I must tell you that

mamma intended to give a grand party. The cards
had been printed, and some of the arrangements
made, but when papa came home he would not hear
a word about it. I have been out quite a good deal
this winter, and have several elegant party dresses.
I was to have a beautiful new pink silk for this, but
mamma would n't buy it when she heard the worst
news. It 's *too* bad ; and if Uncle Edward should be
lame or crippled — O, I cannot bear to think of
it ! If he had been an officer there would have been
a great fuss made about it. I really felt ashamed to
see just ' Edward Meredith, wounded,' as if he were
John Jones, or any common fellow ! But I hope he
will not die. Death is always so gloomy, and mamma would have to wear black ; so there would be an
end to gayeties all the rest of the winter."

Kathie felt rather shocked over this, it sounded so
heartless. Was death only an interruption to pleasure ? As for her, she carried the thought in her
heart day and night, and began to feel what the
Saviour meant when he said, " Pray without ceasing."
How easy it seemed to go to him in any great sorrow !

" But O, is n't it lonely ? " she said to her mother.

"If Uncle Robert had been compelled to go, how could we have endured it?—and Rob away too,—dear Rob!"

That reminded her that she owed him a letter. It was such an effort nowadays to rouse herself to any work of choice or duty. "Which is not marching steadily onward," she thought to herself. "I can only pray for Mr. Meredith, but I may work for others. Rouse thee, little Kathie!"

CHAPTER IX.

THORNS IN THE PATH.

It appeared to **Kathie** that she had never known ᴠ long a fortnight as the first two weeks of Uncle Pobert's absence ; yet everything had gone **on just the same, none of the** duties were **changed, only the** absence and the dreadful **suspense.**

Yet something else had **happened, or was** working **itself out** slowly day by day. Among the new scholars were several quite stylish and fashionable girls, who felt inclined to draw a **line, or** make some kind of a social distinction.

Foremost **among these** was Isabel Hadden, a tall, showy girl, who prided herself **upon her** figure and style. Her **father had made a fortune as an** army contractor, **and was now in** Washington. He had purchased **a very pretty** country residence at Brookside, and installed his **family there,** though Mrs. Hadden **frequently joined him for** weeks at **a time.**

Belle had been at a second-rate boarding-school for a year before the family had attained their present grandeur. Now a distant connection filled the position of governess to the host of younger children ; but Belle considered herself too large to come in with " that crowd," as she rather disdainfully termed them.

She was sent to school every morning in the carriage, and it not infrequently came for her in the afternoon. Rather distant and haughty at first, she had not made friends very easily. Mrs. Thorne happened to meet Mrs. Hadden at an evening party, and it was followed by a mutual acquaintance. Thereupon Isabel and Lottie became friends, though the latter was somewhat younger. Lottie's mother was very ambitious for her, and since Mr. Thorne would not consent to the expense of a boarding-school, she sent Lottie to Mrs. Wilder, as it was so much more genteel.

Belle became the leader of the small clique who discussed fashions habitually. She criticised the dresses, cuffs, collars, and laces for the edification of her youthful hearers, until Emma Lauriston said one day, " Miss Hadden is as good as a fashion-magazine.

I don't know but she would be invaluable in a fancy goods' store."

Lottie still kept to her old habit of calling upon Kathie for assistance when lessons were puzzling. For several days in succession she had occupied Kathie's short intermission, and Mrs. Wilder found that she began to depend too much upon this kindly help.

"Miss Kathie," her teacher said at length, "I have a request or a command in my mind, — you can consider it as which ever is easiest to obey," and Mrs. Wilder smiled.

Kathie smiled as well, in her pleasant fashion.

"I am sorry to find fault with any generous deed that school-girls do for one another, but I think Lottie Thorne has come to depend altogether too much upon you. It is hardly fair to occupy your few moments of recreation when by a little closer application she could solve her own problems and translations. This is really necessary for her own good."

"I did not like to be disobliging," Kathie answered, by way of excuse.

"Your generosity is carried almost to a fault at times. You must learn to say 'No' occasionally."

Kathie's soft eyes were downcast. It *would* be very hard to refuse.

"Lottie has as much **time** to study her lessons at home as you have, and I am always ready to explain any difficulty. That is one of my duties towards my pupils. I am in a measure answerable for her improvement; and if she slips through upon the assistance of others she will be the loser in the end. You understand what I mean?—that while I do not wish to discourage a helpful feeling among the girls, I desire that each one should study for herself."

"Yes," Kathie said, in a low tone.

"And, my little friend, it is necessary that one should learn to be just as well as generous."

Kathie felt the force of the remark. Uncle Robert had explained this occasionally to her in connection with Rob, who was rather fond of making her extensively useful. Then she always hated to say no to others. It was easier to sacrifice her own pleasures or desires.

To smooth the matter for her, Mrs. Wilder. announced that morning that she wished each girl's translations to be exclusively her own work, and if there was any great difficulty she would be glad to have them apply to her.

Kathie left the school-room the instant recess began. Lottie was still puzzling over her algebra, and, having finished that, she took up her imperfect French, meaning to go in search of her little helper.

Two or three girls were discussing a party.

"I helped Hattie Norman make out her list last night," said Belle Hadden. "It is to be very select. Her mother insisted that all the Brookside rabble should not be invited."

Hattie Norman was one of the new-comers. Lottie's heart beat a little faster as she wondered whether she would be classed among the rabble.

"The Norman boys are elegant," pursued Belle. "They have all been to dancing-school; and there will be two of Hattie's cousins from the city, — five young gentlemen of one's own."

"You might tell us who the lucky ones are," pleaded a voice.

"That is *my* secret. The invitations are to be sent out to-day. I would n't miss it for anything. Mamma brought me an elegant tarlatan overskirt the last time she came from New York. It is just a mass of fluted ruffling. I shall wear it over my blue silk, I think; blue is so becoming to me."

Lottie lingered, talking and listening, and before she imagined the moments were half gone the bell on Mrs. Wilder's table rang.

"O Kathie, just stop an instant !" she cried ; but the girls were hurrying in, and somehow Kathie passed on with them.   Fifteen minutes after, the French class was summoned.

"You must write your translation over for to-morrow, Miss Thorne ; and yours, Miss Hadden, is not very perfect ; a little revision would improve it."

Much as she disdained the patient governess at home, Belle found her very useful.

Kathie kept out of Lottie's way.   It looked rather mean to her, but it was better than an open refusal.

The trial came the next day, however.   To Lottie's great delight, she was invited to the party, and her head had been so full of it that all the lessons suffered.   She was casting about in her mind what she could have new, or what could be altered to look like new.

"O Kathie !" she exclaimed at recess, "just help me out with these few lines.   I made so many blunders yesterday, and I was so busy last evening."

"You remember what Mrs. Wilder said on Tuesday." Kathie's heart beat rapidly with the effort, and she felt quite inclined to run away like a little coward.

"What? — O, about asking *her!* but then she never tells one anything. You might, I am sure; or if you will just let me read over your translation."

"It would not be quite fair." Kathie's tone was rather slow and hesitating.

"You need n't be so afraid! I should not copy," was the sharp answer. "Just tell me this case."

One answer surely would not be a crime.

"And this line; I can't make beginning nor end of it."

"I am sorry, Lottie; but Mrs. Wilder said the girls were not to help each other so much, — that each one was to get her own translation — "

"Well, I mean to get my own; I just asked you a question. You are very short and hateful about it!"

"O Lottie, I do not want to disobey Mrs. Wilder! I would help you if I could — if it was right." Kathie uttered the words hurriedly, as if after a moment she should not have the courage to say them at all.

"You are setting up for a saint, we all know; and

it is very convenient to talk about right when one
means to be cross and disobliging ! I would do anything *I* could for a friend, I am sure."

Kathie was silent. She knew by experience that
Lottie had a habit of teasing until she accomplished
her purpose.

" So you really won't do that little favor ? "

" Miss Alston ! " called one of the girls ; and Kathie was glad to go.

Lottie dropped two or three tears of mortification
and disappointment. She had come to depend a
great deal upon Kathie, and it was hard doing without the help. " She is a hateful little thing, after all,"
was her internal comment.

Belle Hadden let her look over her translation
"just a moment." Lottie had a quick eye and a good
memory ; but the lesson was not so perfect that it
could escape Mrs. Wilder's attention.

" Please take a little more pains, Miss Thorne,"
she said ; " I shall have to mark you for both
days."

Coming out of school, they paused, in girl fashion,
to say a few last words. A rather rusty-looking
rockaway wagon passed by, in which were two

females, one of whom was driving. The other
leaned out suddenly, with a cry of joy: "O Miss
Kathie! Mother, stop,—do!"

Kathie colored a little. There was the identical
purple bonnet and red roses, and Sarah Ann had two
long rooster-feathers stuck in her jockey hat, which
certainly were waving in the breeze rather ungrace-
fully; but the child went straight up to the wagon,
thrusting aside the cowardly shame.

"I'm so glad to see you! Do you go to school
there? O my! what a lot of — young ladies!" and
Sarah blushed. "There's the one that laughed at
mother when we were at the Fair! Do you like
her?"

"We are all schoolmates, you know," said Kathie,
in a peculiar, but gentle tone. "Are you well?
This is quite a surprise!"

"You are a good, sensible gal," remarked Mrs.
Strong, with a meaning look, which showed Kathie that she was not so deficient in perception,
after all.

"O yes! How is your uncle? Jim thinks he's
just splendid! We did have such a nice time that
day! I've commenced a long letter to you, and

I 've read both books aloud. We liked the story so much! and I cried over the Evangeline, — I could n't help it. I 'm so glad to have the picture! Was n't it sad?" and the ready tears came into Sarah's eyes.

"It 's a real pleasure to meet you"; and Mrs. Strong's face softened to a motherly glow. "I 've come down to get a cousin whose husband was killed in Tennessee fightin', and the poor thing 's a'most begged her way back with one little child, so I want her to come up and make a good visit while she 's gettin' over the worst. Sez I to father, 'We ain't suffered any from the war, and gettin' good prices all the time for farmin' truck, and it 's a pity if we can't make it a little easier for them who have.' She was such a nice young gal, and used to teach school there at Middleville; but she 's seen sights o' trouble sence. And then Sary Ann begged to come, 'cause her father give her money to buy a new gown."

"And I coaxed mother to go to your house, but she would n't," said Sarah, shyly. "I wanted to hear something about you so much! I 'm so glad!"

"And so am I," returned Kathie, warmly.

Plain and unrefined as Mrs. Strong was, she had a

good, generous heart. "We must not keep Miss Kathie standin' here in the cold," she said. "Which way you goin'?"

"Straight on to Crosby Street."

"I wish you'd jump in and ride."

"O do!" pleaded Sarah.

The girls had pretty well dispersed. Even Emma Lauriston was walking slowly down the street. Kathie declined at first, but they urged so strongly that finally she acceded; and, driving slowly, they had quite a nice talk, though Mrs. Strong insisted upon taking her nearly home, as their shopping was all done.

But the episode had not been suffered to pass unremarked.

"What an elegant turnout!" sneered Belle Hadden. "Some of Kathie Alston's country relations, I suppose."

"No," answered Lottie, "it is some people she met at the Fair."

"What horrid taste, — and what coarse, uncouth creatures! Who *is* Kathie Alston, anyhow? A decided *parvenu*, to my thinking. Are they really rich, — the Alstons?"

11

"No, it is Kathie's uncle, Mr. Conover. He made a fortune off in Australia, I believe. They were poor enough before!" Lottie uttered this rather spitefully. Kathie's refusal to assist her that noon still rankled in her mind.

"Did they live here then?"

"O yes! in one of a row of little cottages; and Mrs. Alston had to sew for a living."

The murder was out. Lottie had a misgiving that this was decidedly mean and treacherous; and yet, she said to herself, it was every word true. Why should the Alstons be ashamed of it? Only it did seem mortifying.

"This is just about what I thought. Kathie Alston has n't a bit of style or dignity; and how they *do* dress her! There was some common linen edging on that ruffle she wore to-day, and I don't believe she ever has more than two dresses at the same time. Plebeian blood will tell. Hattie Norman asked me about them, but I told her Kathie was only a little chit that she would n't care to invite. I don't suppose they let her go to parties, or that she knows how to dance. What is the inside of their house like?"

" It is very beautiful."

" Tawdry and cheap, I fancy. Such people have no taste. There is a great deal in birth. My mother was one of the Van Cortlands, of New York, — real old blue blood ; and I can always tell commoners. I wish there could be some distinction here."

" Mrs. Alston is considered very ladylike," said Lottie, with a touch of remorse.

" By people who are no judges, I suppose. And Mrs. Wilder treats Kathie as if she were the greatest lady in the land ! I think we ought to put her down. Where I went to boarding-school we had two parties, — patricians and plebeians, — and the plebeians were made to keep their places. There ought to be just such a distinction here. The idea of being intimate with a girl whose mother has worked for a living ! Why, we should n't think of recognizing our dressmaker in society !"

This sounded quite grand to foolish Lottie. That *she* was considered good enough to go to the Normans' to a party was a great thing. And then Lottie remembered about some great-grandmother of hers, who had belonged to the French nobility, and escaped during one of the revolutions. Did n't that make her blood a little blue ?• If it would only make the French exercises come easy as well !

Lottie scarcely noticed Kathie the next day. It was rainy, and the "patricians" lingered about the stove, discussing the Norman party. Eight or ten played blind-man's-buff in the walk, and had a gay time, bringing the roses to their cheeks.

Two or three of them had bantered Kathie a little about her "friends," but she accepted it in a very good-natured way.

A day or two after, Emma Lauriston took her drawing over to the window where it was lighter, and still lingered at the table when school closed. Afterward they all fell into a pleasant talk.

"So you have come over to our side," exclaimed Miss Hadden.

"Your side ?" — with a look of surprise.

"Yes, the patricians."

Emma Lauriston had always been called proud, and it was well known that she was to be quite an heiress by and by, her grandmother having left her a considerable fortune.

"I think there can be no question about my tastes or sympathies," she said, rather haughtily. "Refinement, truth, and honor make my nobility."

"Refinement is absolutely necessary to me," remarked Belle, with an elegant air. "Sometimes I am teased about it, but all kinds of coarseness and vulgarity are odious to me, whether it is in dress or behavior. And loud voices or loud manners are equally my detestation."

Emma did not dissent. One or two thoughts of her own took up her attention, and the rest of the talk seemed to float around her like the waves of a distant sea.

Kathie remarked the change very quickly, for she was keenly sensitive. That Lottie should be vexed with her she did not so much wonder at, but why should the other girls shun her? She certainly had done nothing to them. And it gave her a pang to see some small circle fall apart when she joined it, each girl giving knowing glances to the others. Then, too, she was left out of the plays and talks, and though they did nothing absolutely rude, she seemed to understand that there was a kind of social ostracism, and she was being pushed over to the side she did not admire, — to the half-dozen rather coarse girls.

Belle was not slow in spreading abroad the report. The Alstons were mushroom aristocracy. Nobody knew *how* the uncle had made **his** fortune. People did everything in Australia, — robbed, cheated, **even** murdered. And **Mrs.** Alston had actually sewed for a living !

Yet it must be confessed that these very girls **fairly envied her the pony** phaeton and the elegant **house.**

" Uncle Robert is coming home," said her mother, one afternoon. **"We** have received a good long letter from **him, and some** news that will surprise you."

Kathie's face was aglow with interest.

" **You** may read it all yourself. **He** had not time **to write any more than one letter."**

Kathie sat down to her treasure.

" O mamma ! **And Miss** Jessie is married to — **Mr.** Meredith ! **What will** Ada say ? But O, will he never get well ? **It would** be harder than ever to have him **die.** How strange it seems ! Dear Miss Jessie ! "

The doctors **had conquered the fever, but** there **were some** serious complications **with** his wound, **and** he was so reduced that it appeared almost impossible for him to **rally.** Kathie **could** see that Uncle Robert **had very little hope.**

"Still he is very happy and resigned," the letter said. "Since his marriage he seems to have not a wish left ungratified. Mr. and Mrs. George Meredith were present, and the lady was considerably surprised by this unlooked-for termination ; still, she was very gracious to Jessie. But the best of all is his perfect peace and trust. A precious hope the Saviour's love has been, and in his mind his whole brief religious life seems connected with our darling little Kathie. Every day he speaks of her. It is true that God has ordained praise out of the mouths of babes."

The loving messages brought the tears to Kathie's eyes. And most delightful of all was the hope of seeing dear Uncle Robert again. So for two days satirical school shafts fell harmless.

Rob had a flying visit first of all, but the joy at Cedarwood was delightful. Uncle Robert reached home just at dusk, and Kathie could do nothing all the evening but watch him and talk. All the story had to be told over again, and with it many incidents that could not be written, — the heroic bravery, the patient endurance and sweet faith.

"Then he is not sorry that he re-enlisted ?" Kathie asked, anxiously.

"No, my darling. He thinks that his country needed him, and his last act was to procure some very valuable information. He would like to live if it is God's will, but it will be well with him either way."

Uncle Robert held the little hand in his and gave it a fond pressure. Kathie knew what it said, but her heart felt very humble.

The next morning she had to tell him about Sarah Strong.

"And how kind it is in Mrs. Strong to take home this poor cousin!" Kathie said. "I liked her manner of speaking of it so much. But I think — "

Kathie made a long pause.

"A remarkable thought it must be!" said her uncle, smiling.

Fred ran in to have his pencil sharpened, and also to announce that one of the cunning little guinea-pigs was dead. So Kathie's school discomfort passed out of her mind.

But it met her on the threshold again. She was rather early at school, as Uncle Robert wished to drive about the village to do several errands.

Half a dozen girls were discussing tableaux. Kathie joined them with a face full of interest.

"O," she exclaimed, "I do love to hear about tableaux! Are you really going to have them?"

There was a coolness and silence in the small circle.

"It was a little matter of our own that we were discussing," said Belle Hadden, loftily.

Kathie turned. She had been in such a happy mood that she was ready for anything. And the two or three experiences in tableaux had left such a delightful memory that she was fain to try it again.

She went to her seat quietly. The voices floated dimly over to her.

"It is mean not to ask her!"

"Girls, I know Mrs. Wilder will notice it, and speak of it."

"You can all do as you like, but if you want Tom, Dick, and Harry, and everybody in them, I beg leave to be excused," said a rather sharp, haughty voice.

"But Kathie Alston is n't —"

"I would as soon have Mary Carson, or any one of that class. They are all alike."

Mary Carson's father had made a fortune in buying and selling iron. She was as coarse as Sarah Strong, without her ambition or good, tender heart.

Somehow Kathie rebelled at being placed in the same category. She took up her book and tried to study, but her heart was swelling with a sense of injustice. What had she done to these girls? She was not coarse, or vulgar, or mean.

"Plebeian and patrician," some one said with a laugh, as they dispersed at Mrs. Wilder's entrance.

Kathie heard of the plan through the course of the day. Some of the larger girls had proposed that they should give a little entertainment for the benefit of the wife and children of a Captain Duncan who had been killed in one of the recent battles. Mrs. Duncan was staying at Brookside, quite prostrated by her misfortunes.

Thirteen of the school-girls had been asked. Mrs. Coleman, Mrs. Duncan's warmest friend, had offered her parlor and dining-room. Sue Coleman was hand and glove with Belle Hadden.

Now and then Kathie glanced over to Mary Carson. Vulgarity was written in every line of her broad, freckled face. Something beside plainness, — snub nose, wiry brown hair, and the irregular teeth, which looked as if they were never brushed, — an air of self-sufficiency, as if she considered herself as good as the best. She was continually talking of what they had at home, and made the most absurd blunders, which Mrs. Wilder patiently corrected. The small satires of the other girls never pierced the armor of her complacency. "And they think me like her!" Kathie mused, with a sad, sore heart. "I suppose because our fortune came so suddenly; and yet mamma always was a lady. However, I must bear it patiently."

Uncle Robert, seeing her so grave, fancied that it was on account of Mr. Meredith; and he was so busy that for a few days they had no confidential talks.

It was very hard to feel so entirely alone. Even Emma Lauriston was at home sick with a sore throat.

CHAPTER X.

UNDER FIRE.

EMMA LAURISTON was absent from school three days, and then took her place, looking somewhat pale and languid; but several of the girls were rather impatient to see her.

"Have you heard bad news?" she asked of Kathie. "My cousin said your uncle had returned."

"Yes," in a grave tone, rather unlike the sunshiny Kathie.

"That was quite a romance about your friend Miss Darrell. Do they think Mr. Meredith will — never get well?"

"They are afraid."

The little bell sounded to call them to order, and then began the usual lessons. Kathie's were always perfect, and yet, oddly enough, it seemed to Emma that her whole heart was not in them.

She had fallen into the habit of watching Kathie very narrowly. The " something different from other

girls " was still a puzzle to her; and when the doctor
had said, a few days ago, " You just missed having a
severe attack of diphtheria," it startled Emma a good
deal. She knew several who had died of diphtheria;
and if she were to die —

Of course she wanted to live. She was young,
and full of hope; and there would be the fortune by
and by, — one of those odd bequests of which she
reaped little benefit now, as it was to go on accumu-
lating until she was twenty-one; but then she would
be able to do a great many delightful things with it.
That was not all, however. There was something
very terrible in the idea of death.

" O Miss Lauriston, we have ever so much to tell
you and to talk about!" exclaimed Sue Coleman.
" We are going to have some tableaux for a charita-
ble object, and we want you to stand in several of
them. You will make such a lovely Sister of Charity
in Consolation."

With that the ball was fairly opened. Emma was
pleased and interested at once.

" You are all to come over to my house after
school. Belle Hadden has planned everything. She
is a host in herself."

Kathie had been walking up and down with two
or three girls that she did not care much about, only
they had joined her, and were, perhaps, better company than her lonely thoughts.

"You are going over to Mrs. Coleman's, — are you
not?" asked Emma, in surprise. "Don't you like
tableaux?"

"Very much, but — Good by"; and Kathie made
a feint of kissing her hand.

"Girls, have n't you asked Kathie Alston?" exclaimed Emma, in the first lull, for the talk had been
very energetic; "she would make up lovely in ever
so many characters."

There was a silence, and the girls glanced at each
other with determination in their faces.

"What is the matter? Has she offended you? I
noticed something a little peculiar in school to-day."

"Kathie Alston is well enough — in her place."

Emma colored. "Her place is as good as any of
ours, I suppose," she made answer, slowly.

"Well, I don't quite think it is"; and Belle took up
the glove. "There are some social distinctions —"
The rest of the sentence was rather troublesome.

"I am sure the Alstons are rich, if that is what
you mean."

"That is not altogether what I mean"; yet Belle was a trifle embarrassed at being forced to meet the issue so squarely, though every girl felt in her secret soul that Emma was undeniably aristocratic. "If we are to take up everybody who becomes suddenly rich, there is Mary Carson and several others; and I 've never been used to it. Mamma *is* particular about my associates."

"But the Alstons are educated, refined, and were always wealthy until they met with a reverse of fortune when Mr. Alston died."

"And Mrs. Alston used to sew for the whole neighborhood, I 've heard. Fancy being compelled to meet your seamstress as an — an equal! Mrs. Wilder ought to be more exclusive about her scholars. Mamma said so herself. And only a few days ago some horrid country clowns stopped right in front of the school, and she went off to take a ride in their forlorn old wagon. Our cook is actually related to these people! Their name is Strong, — a coarse, vulgar set, I know."

Belle talked very rapidly, and her face flushed with excitement. For several moments Emma hesitated. The distinction appeared paltry and mean to her.

Then she really *did* like Kathie. "Girls," she began, at length, "I think you are unjust. I have been at Cedarwood, and met all the family. They are refined, intelligent, have a lovely home, and are — truly noble and Christian people." Emma uttered the last in spite of herself.

"Well, every one can do as she likes"; and Belle gave her head a haughty toss. "I don't think because a man digs up a nugget of gold in Australia he is entitled to a king's position at once. There are some girls at school that I should not associate with under *any* circumstances."

Emma had a feeling that this was really absurd; yet most of the girls had ranged themselves on this side, and it did require a good deal of courage to go against the opinions of her mates and friends. Still, when she came to think of it, Mrs. Grayson visited the Alstons, the Darrells were their firm friends, and that rich and elegant Mr. Meredith! But Kathie *was* rather inclined to be hand and glove with people beneath her.

"And Kathie Alston *does* take up everybody," said one of the girls. "Every few days you see her having some common thing in that pony-phaeton of hers.

She has n't a bit of pride or good taste, and it seems to me that is next of kin to refinement."

" Let us go on with the tableaux."

Emma listened to the arrangements in silence. This made such a beautiful scene, — that was so brilliant, or so pathetic, and must not be left out. And before they were aware the dusky evening dropped down about them.

" Girls," she said at length, in a soft, low voice, " I have decided that I will not take part in the tableaux. Kathie Alston and I have been friends, and I shall do nothing that I am quite sure to be ashamed of afterward. You have been very kind to ask me, and I am not angry with any of the opinions I have heard expressed, though they may not please me. Good night."

" Let her go over to the plebeians !" said some one, with a laugh.

At home Kathie had two pleasant surprises. First, a letter from Miss Jessie all to herself, in which they hoped, very faintly indeed, that Mr. Meredith had taken a turn for the better. If the good news should prove true, they meant, as soon as it would be safe, to remove to a private house. And then she said,

12

" My darling little Kathie, we often feel that we would give half the world to see you."

The other was from Sarah, — a decided improvement upon her Christmas epistle, — not a word misspelled, and the sentences very fairly constructed. The last part was filled with Cousin Ellen and her little boy. Sarah told the whole story in her innocence, without the least intention of boasting. Mr. and Mrs. Strong had offered these poor wayfarers a home until they could do better.

" It is very good of them, — is n't it ? " said Kathie. " If the Strongs are not polished, they have generous hearts."

" It certainly is most kind ; and I am wonderfully pleased with the improvement in Sarah."

" Uncle Robert, would it be rude to send Sarah a pretty blue hair-ribbon, and tell her a little about contrasting colors ? I wish she would not wear so much scarlet. Is it wrong for everybody to look as pretty as he or she can ? "

" No, my dear ; and sometimes a delicate hint proves very useful. Sarah has entirely too much color for scarlet ; she needs something to tone her down."

Kathie had been casting about for some time how to manage this matter nicely, and her present idea appeared both delicate and feasible to her. Looking over her store, she found a fresh, pretty ribbon, and forgot all about the school trouble.

The tableaux progressed rapidly. A number of the Academy boys were invited to join. Mr. Coleman had some tickets printed, which sold rapidly, and the affair promised to be successful.

But one evening Dick Grayson said, "Emma Lauriston would look prettier in Consolation, and make the best Evangeline, of any girl in Brookside. Why have n't you asked her and Kathie Alston ? "

" Emma declined," was the almost abrupt answer.

" But Kathie is the sweetest little girl I ever saw. She is always ready for everything."

There was no response. Belle Hadden had gone quite too far to admit that *her* line of distinction had been wrongly drawn. Lottie Thorne felt both sorry and ashamed; but there was no going back without a rather humiliating admission. And yet if she only had *not* spoken that day !

But Emma and Kathie drew nearer together in a quiet way through these troubled times. There were some petty slights to endure, and many unkindnesses. Friends and companions can wound each other so often in a noiseless manner,— pain and sting without the buzzing of a wasp, so patent to all the world,— and I often think these unseen hurts are the hardest to bear.

The evening at Mrs. Coleman's was both delightful and profitable. The Brookside Standard contained quite a glowing account of the entertainment, and praised the young ladies for their labor in so good a cause. The sum received, with several donations, amounted to eighty-seven dollars.

"Why did you not speak of it, Kathie?" asked Uncle Robert. "We would all have gone."

Now, there had not been even a ticket offered to Kathie. Indeed, the space being limited, Sue and Belle had made out a list of guests beforehand.

Kathie colored violently, and Uncle Robert looked quite astonished. Seeing that she was expected to answer, she summoned her courage.

"It was a — a party affair of the larger girls in school. They did not ask every one."

"But we might have sent a gift, the object was so very worthy."

Kathie made no reply to that. Uncle Robert studied the grave face, and decided that something had gone wrong.

Dick Grayson dropped in that evening. " I was so disappointed about your not being there," he said. " You would just have fitted in two or three of the tableaux."

But Kathie did not appear to be disposed to converse on the subject, so they wandered off into a talk about Rob, and then Mr. Meredith claimed their attention.

The patricians flourished in grand style. It would have been really laughable to sensible people to see how one after another copied Belle Hadden's airs and graces, and how the gulf widened in school. Several of the girls asked to have their seats changed, until the plebeians were left quite to themselves.

And yet the matter worked out a very odd and rather mortifying retaliation. One afternoon Dick Grayson overtook Emma Lauriston walking homeward. He had that day received a letter from her brother Fred, and repeated some of the contents.

" Are you going to Belle Hadden's party?" he asked, presently.

"I have not had any invitation." Emma's tone was rather curt.

"No?" in the utmost surprise. "What has happened among you girls? You and Kathie were not at the tableaux. Is there a standing quarrel?"

Dick and Emma were excellent friends in boy-and-girl fashion.

"There is something very mean and foolish. I wish somebody could look at it with clear eyes and give Belle Hadden a lesson!"

Emma's usually soft voice was indignant, and her face crimsoned with excitement.

"But how did Kathie Alston come to get mixed up with it. It seems to me that she is the last one to quarrel."

"There was no quarrel, at least no words. There are some very aristocratic girls in school, and Belle is forever talking about her mother's family. So they have divided the girls into patricians and plebeians."

"But Mr. Conover is a gentleman, and the Alstons are all refined. The idea of putting Kathie on the plebeian side is absurd! And you too —"

"I went over there," she said, sharply. "I would not take part in the tableaux on that account.

Kathie had done nothing to them. It was because her mother used to sew, I believe, and then Kathie herself is not a bit proud. I suppose if they made a great show and parade like the Haddens —"

"I did not think Belle was that small! And you are a splendid champion, Emma. But Kathie is worthy of the best friendship in the world. She is never mean or envious, or looking out for the best places, and Mr. Conover is just royal. The idea of the Haddens setting themselves up! Why, Mrs. Alston used to sew for my mother, and mother is one of her warmest friends. Is n't there something very unjust about girls, — some girls, I mean ?" blushing as he corrected himself. "And why does not Mrs. Wilder interfere, or is she on the patrician side ?"

"Mrs. Wilder really does n't know anything about it. The little hateful acts are done on the sly, just looks and tones, or some sentence that no one can take hold of. It would seem silly to complain of not being noticed. But it takes away the pleasant feeling that used to exist."

"And how does Kathie bear it ?"

"Like a little angel. It hurts her cruelly too. About the time this first began, some very common-

looking people spoke to Kathie in the street, and
the girls have laughed and sneered at that. ·Indeed,
nothing that she does escapes them. I almost wish
that I was n't a girl!"

"Boys don't badger a fellow that way, if they did
there would be some thrashing! But I know just
how to come up with Belle Hadden, and I 'll do it!"

With that Dick laughed.

Emma was so much exasperated that the thought
rather delighted her.

"What will you do?"

"I can't tell you until afterward. Don't I wish
Rob Alston was home, though! He would enjoy
the fun."

They separated at Emma's gate. She was not altogether sure that she was right in her desire, but she
determined not to worry herself on that score.

Belle's party was to be quite a grand affair. A
number of the Academy boys were invited, those
who were rich and stylish; Belle did not come to
school the next day, and the girls were rather in-
discreet without their leader.

The rooms were beautiful, the supper elegant, the
music fine, but — there were so *few* young gentle-

men ! Not Dick Grayson, nor Walter Dorrance, nor Charlie Darrell, nor — ever so many others that had been counted upon sure.

Emma guessed as she heard the floating talk.

" I do suppose Belle Hadden was as deeply mortified last night as she could be," Emma said to Kathie. ' If ever I have another cause that I want righted I will place it in Dick Grayson's hand. He is equal to Arthur's knights."

" What did he do ? "

" He said he had a plan. I know now that it must have been to keep the nicest boys away from the party. Belle likes Dick so much too. It must have been worth seeing, — their disappointment. A host of wall-flowers with no one to lead them out to dance !"

" You did n't ask him to do it ? " Kathie's face was full of pain and regret.

" No, not exactly. Indeed, I did not know *what* he meant to do, only I was telling him about Belle Hadden's meanness, and he thought of a way to pay her back."

" I am so sorry it was — that way."

" Kathie !"

"O Emma dear, don't think me ungrateful! You have stood by me of your own accord, I know," and Kathie clasped her hand. "I am so much obliged to you. They had nothing against you at first, and they were very sorry not to have you at the tableaux. But it always troubles me to know that other people have suffered — "

"Not when they deserve it, surely !"

"Always — if it can be helped."

"And you would not have done this ? You think it was not right for me to tell ?"

What could Kathie say, — blame her brave comrade ?

"No, you do not think it right. I can see that in your face ! Kathie, how *can* you bear everything so patiently ?"

"God makes it all right at last. He asks us to wait his time. And though it is very hard — " Kathie's lip quivered and her voice grew unsteady.

"It seems to me this has been the meanest thing I ever knew. You cannot guess what gave it the first start."

"Yes. It was while you were sick that the girls — took a dislike to me. I spoke to some people one day, some friends," correcting herself, "and Belle laughed at them. Then the girls talked about — mamma."

"It was shameful!"

"We *were* poor, and we had to work. Mamma could not help all that. And then Uncle Robert came, and we have been so very happy ever since. Thinking of it all, I don't mind this little trouble much. All that Belle says cannot make us coarse and vulgar and ignorant, and I have been trying all the time to look on the best and brightest side."

Emma put her arm suddenly around Kathie.

"What is it," she asked, in a husky voice, — "what is it that makes you sweet and patient and tender and forgiving, always ready to minister to others and to the poor, even if you are laughed at and teased? Maybe it's the same grace that takes away the fear of death! O, I wish I knew! I wish I had it! I am sometimes so miserable, Kathie. Do you believe that your God *could* love and pity me a little?"

"'Him that cometh to me I will in no wise cast out.'"

It was all that Kathie could think of to say as Emma stopped short in her walk, trembling, excited, and tearful.

" But how to come ? "

Kathie hesitated.   It seemed that she knew so
little herself, how then could she direct another ?
She remembered the other time when she failed to
bear witness, and though her shy, delicate nature
shrank from anything like a parade of her most
sacred feelings, strength was given her when she
asked for it.

" I do not know how it is always — " in her sweet,
faltering voice, " but when I first wanted to try — to
be good, — to follow HIM even a little, it was just as
if I reached out my hand and prayed him to take it,
and kept close to him by endeavoring to do what he
wishes — "

" And you did not have — any great light — "

" I had only a love and a desire to obey him.
And it seemed as if everybody helped me, — mamma, Aunt Ruth, and Uncle Robert.   But there is
always something to overcome, some battle to fight.

" And I am a poor, raw recruit.   Do you think
He will accept me, Kathie ? "

" Every one — to the uttermost."

They walked to the corner, where their paths di-
verged.

"I wish you would come and see me," Kathie said, with her ready grace. " Fred was there occasionally last summer, and Uncle Robert liked him so much ! "

" And you will forgive that — revenge ? Perhaps I ought to have waited."

Kathie's look was sufficient, though she could not have spoken.

But the child went home in a gravely sweet frame of mind. She was in a mood to tell Uncle Robert the whole story that evening ; but there were several guests, so there could be no confidences.

The next morning, after school was opened, Mrs. Wilder rose and told them she had a few words to say upon a subject that had been a source of much disquiet for several days ; and then she very kindly but wisely took up the matter that had so divided and agitated the girls, and severely condemned the folly of which some of them had been guilty. " They would find as they grew older," she said, " that with people of culture and refinement social distinctions did not depend so much on a little more or a little less money, but nobleness of soul, thought, and feeling, — deeds that could brave and endure the scrutiny of clear eyes, and not those which must always slink away and hide themselves behind whispered insinuations."

It seemed, after all, as if, in some mysterious way, Mrs. Wilder had learned all the particulars. She mentioned no names, and did not in the least seek to exalt Kathie; but the child knew by the kiss and the lingering glance bestowed upon her that afternoon that all her silence and pain had been appreciated.

If Belle needed anything further to lower her self-esteem, she had it on her return home. Mr. Conover, Mrs. Alston, and Mrs. Grayson had met at the house of a mutual friend when Mrs. Hadden happened to call.

"Belle," she began, sharply, "how could you have committed such a blunder as to omit that pretty little Miss Alston from your party-list? Her mother and her uncle are very charming people, and they have a host of elegant friends in New York. Mrs. Havens was here last summer to visit them, and those aristocratic Merediths are warm friends of theirs. I am so sorry it should have happened!"

"Miss Alston is a regular little Methodist, — too good to go to parties," returned Belle, rather crossly.

And so ended the reign of the patricians. Belle somehow lost prestige at school. Even Lottie began to be pleasant again with Kathie, secretly hoping that Belle would never repeat her unlucky remark.

Dick Grayson and Charlie had to tell Kathie one evening how they spoiled a good deal of the fun at Belle Hadden's party.

"I felt so sorry," Kathie said, gravely.

"Well, you are the queerest girl I ever saw," was Charlie's comment; yet something inside told him she was a noble one as well.

But the sweetest of all was the talk with Uncle Robert.

CHAPTER XI.

IN ANOTHER'S STEAD.

CLOSER pressed the ranks of brave men who were to strike a final blow for the good cause, nearer, nearer, marching on with a steady, crushing step. The nation rejoiced over victories, but firesides, from palace to hovel, missed and mourned some dear, familiar face, some cheerful voice that would never speak again.

Kathie used to watch daily. The campaign was growing more exciting as it approached the end. Her heart used to beat chokingly as she glanced down the lists. And this was what she saw one day: "Missing, William Morrison."

"O mamma!" with a quick cry, "did you read this?"

Mrs. Alston looked. "Oh!" she exclaimed, with sudden pain. "Uncle Robert and Mr. Morrison have gone to the nursery to select a few more fruit-trees. They will doubtless hear of it at the village."

" You do not think — he has been — killed !"

Kathie's face was very pale and her sweet voice faltered.

" Hardly," returned Mrs. Alston. " But one can never be quite certain what becomes of the missing."

Kathie put on her shawl and hood presently, and walked slowly down the winding drive. She had not sufficient courage to enter the cottage, though through the window she saw Ethel and Jamie having a game of romps. The child's cheeks were like roses, and now and then a careless laugh floated out to Kathie, who shivered with something more than cold.

Presently the wagon approached slowly. When Uncle Robert caught sight of his little niece he sprang out and greeted her warmly.

" I have some good news for you, Kitty," he said, in his bright, breezy tone. " Mr. Meredith is really better. They hope to bring him home before long. Why — is n't it delightful ?" seeing that she made no answer.

" Yes, I am very, very thankful."

" But, Kathie — what has happened, little one ? "

" Our other soldier — "

13

"Mr. Morrison — O child, what tidings of him?"

"There has been another battle, and he is — missing."

"The news might be worse then. There is a little hope, so do not despair at once."

Kathie grasped his arm tighter, and they walked nearly to the house in silence. Then he said, "Of what are you thinking, my darling?"

There were tears in her soft, violet eyes.

"Uncle Robert, what a strange and solemn thing it is to have any one die for you, — in your stead."

"Yes. I wonder if we do not sometimes forget the One who died eighteen hundred years ago? But this brings it home to you and me in a manner that we shall always remember."

"And, looking at that, all our little trials and burdens seem as nothing. I thought it quite hard to be treated so unjustly at school, but what was it compared with giving up one's life?"

"It is something, my darling, when we bear reviling from that highest of all motives, — His sake. Even the little steps are precious in his sight. We are not all called upon to walk the sorrowful way he trod."

" But poor little Ethel !"

" We promised, you know, to make all the amends in our power to her."

" But it seems to me that nothing could comfort me if you were gone."

He took the cold little face in his hands, as they were standing on the broad porch now, at the very door.

"Do you love me so well, my child? But we must not forget that those who stay at home are sometimes called from the earthly ranks. God asks of us that his will and pleasure shall be ours as well."

" Yes, I know "; but her voice was quite faint as he kissed her.

It was dusk, and as he opened the door the cheerful light and warmth of the hall were most grateful. Kathie gave a shiver as if she were shaking off the wintry cold.

" Do not anticipate the worst," he said, pleasantly. " To-morrow's news may be different."

She smiled faintly. " I am not a very good soldier, after all," she returned, with a little faltering in her tones.

"My darling, when our Captain calls us out to fight, he always gives us grace and strength. But we must never look away from him; that is part of the promise." .

She hung up her hood, smoothed her hair, that had been blown about by the wind, and went in to supper. They all talked a little about Mr. Morrison, but it appeared to Kathie that they were wonderfully hopeful. Indeed, the news from Mr. Meredith was so very encouraging that it seemed to dim the force of the other.

Afterward Mr. Conover went down to the cottage. Freddy brought his solitaire-board to Kathie.

"I've forgotten how it is done," he said, "and I want you to show me. Let me take them out, and you just tell me when I go wrong."

It really seemed that Fred had a marvellous faculty for going wrong. Kathie felt very much as if she did not care to be bothered. She was restless and nervous, and wanted to curl herself up on Aunt Ruth's lounge and think a little.

"Greater love hath no man —" the words kept running through her mind. But the love began in little things, even the love which suffered at last upon the cross. So she roused herself to patience and interest.

Uncle Robert looked quite grave when he returned. The Morrisons had heard the tidings, and were very anxious.

"I must write to Mr. Morrison's captain to-morrow," he said. "We must make every effort to find him. He may have been wounded and carried off of the field unnoticed."

Kathie prayed fervently for Mr. Morrison's safety. Uncle Robert made immediate inquiries, and they waited in half fear, half hope. In the mean while events in Virginia had the stirring ring of near victories. All was breathless excitement throughout the land. Sorties, surprises, battles, Sherman coming up from his march to the sea, Sheridan brave and dashing as ever, and Grant going slowly with his men, like some ponderous machine that was to crush at last.

And then the telegraph flashed the news far and wide: "Lee has surrendered!" "Richmond has been taken!"

It seemed so odd to Kathie to be going on in her quiet, uneventful fashion. School lessons, music

practices, **home** duties, — nothing grand or heroic.
Mrs. Wilder's lecture to the **girls had** been produc-
tive of a little good, beside breaking the foolish cabal;
for in it she had touched upon dress and parties, and
tried to set before them the urgency of paying some
attention to their studies. So there were fewer bows,
a plainer arrangement of hair, and less talk of
fashion.

"I **think it** was **mean to** crowd Kathie Alston
out," declared Sue Coleman. "Mamma says the Alstons **are** people one might be proud of anywhere;
and they are extremely well connected. She met
them one evening at Mrs. Adams's, and that elegant
Mr. Langdon thinks Mr. Conover about perfect.
Mamma is so sorry that we did not have her in
the tableaux. **Every** one noticed **it.** That was your
fault, Belle!"

"**Of course** you are all quite at liberty to choose
your **own friends,**" Belle answered, loftily; "I'm sure
you agreed **to it. You did** not want Mary Carson
and all that rabble."

"Mary and Kathie are not friends in our accepta-
tion of the **term.** She is **polite to** Mary, and **I am
not sure but** that a ladylike courtesy is more effec-

tual in keeping people at a distance than absolute rudeness. I believe Kathie and Emma Lauriston are the only two girls in the school who have not indulged in rudeness in some form or other."

"If she is not hand and glove with Mary Carson, she has another friend who is no better, whom she visits and sends pictures to, and I don't know what all. It's a second or third cousin of our cook. Of course these Strongs are rich; so it is not the breeding as much as the money. But, as I said, you can all do as you like. It seems to me that half of the town has gone crazy on the subject of Kathie Alston."

Emma was a little troubled with these talks about Sarah Strong. She had a certain delicacy which held her aloof from any such associations. "Kathie," she said at length, "I wish you would tell me how you came to take a fancy to those people who were at — the Fair, I believe."

Kathie colored a little. "I don't know as you would understand it," she answered, slowly.

"I am beginning to comprehend some things," her eyes drooping a little, and glancing past Kathie.

"I noticed them at the Fair — because — something was said to hurt their feelings — "

"O, I know ! Lottie Thorne came over to our table and made fun of the woman. But — do you not think — such people always take advantage of a little notice ? — and then it leads to mortifying embarrassments."

" Maybe that is just one of the things God puts in the daily warfare to make us good soldiers. It is like being a private in the army. Sometimes people sneer at the hard, rough work the soldiers have to do, and yet it often helps the officers to gain the victory."

"And the officers have the credit. That looks rather unjust, does n't it ? "

"It would seem hard if God did not remember it all."

" But how did you come to visit the Strongs ? "

Kathie told the whole story. "I cannot explain these things to you just as Uncle Robert does," she went on, with a rather perplexed smile. "Always when I am in any doubt or trouble I go to him. He thinks when people are anxious for mental or social improvement a helping hand does them so much good. Persons in their own station cannot give it, as a general thing. And the Saviour said,

THE COMFORTER. — Page 203.

'Inasmuch as ye have done it unto the least of these —' "

" Yes, I see. But it is harder to do your good in that way, Kathie."

" Digging in the trenches"; and Kathie smiled.

" Ah, you have gone out as a private in the ranks; and I am afraid, after all, that very few of us like to be privates," Emma returned. " But it certainly did show a good deal of delicate feeling and remembrance when Sarah Strong sent you the lichen."

" I thought so. And our visit was very pleasant."

" Only, if she had not spoken to you that day in the street, it would have saved you a good deal of pain and trouble," returned Emma.

" Maybe it was just what I needed. Life is so pleasant and lovely to me that I might forget who gives it all if every once in a while something did not bring me back to Him. And it is so good, when others misunderstand and blame, to know that God sees all, and never makes a mistake in his judgment."

Emma was silent. It was the keeping near to Him that rendered Kathie meek, patient, and full of love. And it seemed to Emma as if she strayed continually.

Was it because Kathie always had some good work in hand?

But amid all the rejoicing, and the certainty that Mr. Meredith would recover, the other shadow seemed to be growing deeper. Three weeks, and not a word of Mr. Morrison yet. His captain remembered the man, and could only account for the disappearance by supposing that he had been buried among the rebel dead. Twice since the battle they had exchanged prisoners, and he had not been returned among the well or wounded; and now every one was flocking to the Union lines.

"Mr. Darrell went to Washington to-day," Uncle Robert announced to Kathie. "He is to bring Jessie and Mr. Meredith home."

"Here, — to Brookside?"

"Yes," with a smile. "He needs the quiet and the country air, and I fancy there are two or three people here whom he is longing to see."

Kathie's heart beat with a great bound.

By and by she found herself rambling slowly toward the cottage. Hugh was busy with some spring preparations, pruning trees and vines. He nodded to her, but did not seem inclined to stop and

talk, and Jamie caught hold of her dress, begging her
to come in.

Grandmother took off her spectacles and wiped
them; she often did this now, for her eyes grew dim
many times a day.

" So you have had good news," she said, after the
first greeting. " I am glad there is a little joy saved
out of the great wreck. Such a handsome young
man as Mr. Meredith was too; but there 's many
a bonny lad sleeping under the sod, who was fair
enough to his mother."

Kathie slipped her hand within the one so wrin-
kled and trembling.

" It is such a sorrow to us all," she said, in her
soft, comforting tone. " I keep thinking of it day and
night. It was so noble in him to go — to suffer —"

" It is the one thing, Miss Kathie, that gives me a
little resignation. I shall always feel thankful that
he went in your dear uncle's stead, not for the money
merely. And if it has saved him — if it has kept
you all together; but this is too sad a talk for you,
dear child."

The tears were dropping from Kathie's long bronze
lashes.

"Dear grandmother, there has not been a morning nor night but that I have remembered him and his generous deed. I know his life was as precious to you as Uncle Robert's was to us, and now poor little Ethel is an orphan — for my sake. How strange that the whole world keeps doing for one another, and that, after all, no one really stands alone in it!"

"We are nearer than we think for — rich and poor, when one takes God's word aright. We can't any of us do without the other unless there comes a sense of loss and something that is not quite right. You and yours see further into it than most folk. I 'm glad to have the precious comfort of knowing that William went safely, and that in the other country he has met his dear wife. I shall soon go to them, and I know well that little Ethel will never lack for friends. William felt it with great certainty."

Another duty was laid upon Kathie. This orphan was to be more to her than any chance friend. What could she do of her own self? Only to show her now how truly she appreciated the sacrifice and loss, and to put a few simple pleasures in her life, to give her tenderness and affection that might make some slight amends.

She thought of something else that evening.

"Uncle Robert," she said, "do you believe there is any hope that Mr. Morrison may still be alive?"

"It is very slight now," he answered. "And yet I can hardly be reconciled to the loss amid this general rejoicing. It seems so much harder to have him dead now that the war is over and many of the soldiers will soon return home."

"I feel so sorry that he had to die out there alone. If some one could have given him only a cup of cold water — "

"Perhaps they did."

"But if it had been you!" Kathie clung closely to him as if there might be danger yet.

"It was not, my darling. God seems to hold me in the hollow of his hand, and while he takes such care of me I feel more than ever the need of doing his work. And now little Ethel has been added to us."

"Uncle Robert, I think I ought to take a special share in it, since God has left me the delight of your love."

"As Ethel grows older, there will be many things that you can do."

"But I have thought of this one now. The interest on Ethel's little fortune amounts to almost one hundred dollars."

"A little more than that. I put it in bonds."

"And if it could be saved for her, — since she will want but very little. She will have her home with her aunt, and need only her clothes. I 'd like to buy those for her as a kind of thank-offering."

"But, my darling, in a few years more you will be a young lady, and there will come parties, journeys, and pleasures of different kinds, where it may be necessary for you to be dressed in something besides the simple garments of childhood. Perhaps you will want more money yourself!"

"I never have to give up anything needful, but I was thinking that I should like now and then to make a real sacrifice, relinquish some article that I wanted very much, and use it for her instead. It would help me to remember what her father had done for me."

Uncle Robert stooped and kissed her, touched to the heart by her simple act of self-denial.

"It shall be as you wish," he replied, tenderly. "And, my dear child, I am glad to see you willing to take your share in the great work there is to be done in the world."

"It is so little, after all, and so many blessings come to me."

Ah, was it not true that God restored fourfold? After many days the bread we have cast upon the waters comes floating back to us. Well for us then if we are not shamed by niggardly crumbs and crusts flung out impatiently to some wayside beggar while we ourselves feasted. For God's work and love go together, and there is always something for the willing hand.

CHAPTER XII.

HOME AGAIN.

THE pony phaeton stood before the school-house, Jasper and Hero nodding their heads impatiently in the April sunshine. The prettiest striped lap-robe imaginable was thrown over the empty seat, the plating of the harness made a silvery glitter, and altogether it was a turnout that one might be rather proud of, if one's self-complacency was nurtured upon such things.

And the driver thereof was not to be despised. The girls, as they trooped down stairs, thought Kathie Alston "so lucky!" No one in Brookside had a father or uncle or brother so devoted, — not old, by any means, and certainly good-looking, but, best of all, showing his affection in a manner that made her envied of others.

Sue Coleman had met him several times through the course of the winter, and pronounced him " magnificent," in her enthusiastic fashion. Indeed, he was

the kind of man to be very attractive to young girls.
She bowed now in her most gracious manner. Belle
bit her lip angrily. If she had taken up Kathie
instead of that insignificant little gossiping Lottie
Thorne! Her mother had been to call at Cedarwood, but it was n't at all likely that she would be
invited within its charmed precincts. Of course she
said she did not care; but there was a gnawing jeal-
ousy at her heart.

Uncle Robert was so in the habit of coming for
Kathie that she sprang in, nodded a gay farewell
to the group, and went on for some distance before
she thought it anything more than a pleasure drive.

Suddenly her heart gave a quick bound. "You
are going to the Darrells'?" she said.

"Yes." Disguise it as he might, there was a glow
in the half-averted eyes.

"O, Mr. Meredith has n't — come home!"

"Has n't he? Are you quite sure?" — with a
little smile.

"O Uncle Robert!"

"They came at twelve. I was in there half an
hour, when he insisted that I should drive over for
you."

14

It was very flattering to be remembered first of all; and yet there was something connected with it which made Kathie's heart beat in an unwonted manner, and a quiver came into her throat almost as if she wanted to cry. Six months ago! — how much had happened since then!

He fastened the horses, and entered the hall with Kathie, who seemed strangely shy.

"They took him right up to Miss Jessie's room," said her uncle.

Thither they went, though there was a sound of joyous voices in grandmother's room, just across the hall. The two halted a moment, then Uncle Robert pushed the door a little wider open.

" Have you brought her ? "

The dear, well-known voice, sounding a bit husky and tremulous, and with something in it which brought the tears to Kathie's eyes. What with the flood of sunshine, the white bed and pillows a little tumbled, and a gray travelling-wrap thrown partly over somebody, she seemed to see nothing but confusion at first; then a thin white hand was stretched out.

"I am so tired that I cannot rise. Dear Kathie! Dear child!"

They were both crying then, and neither felt ashamed. Just a miracle that he was here at all; and if he had gone to the other country, the golden key opening the gates set with jasper and pearl must have been Kathie's precious words.

"My dear Kathie, I've lost all the little sense I ever did have. I sent Jessie away for fear she might indulge in a scene, and here I am crying like a baby! But there are so many things to think of, and it is so delightful to see familiar faces once more!"

Then Kathie took a look at him. He was very thin and pale, the hair and beard cropped quite close, the eyes sunken, yet with the old bright glow she had watched so many times; and, oddest of all, the once plump hands looking, as Hannah would have said, like "chickens' claws."

"Well, should you know me?"

"Yes, but you are changed."

"And if you had seen me a month ago! The doctors have cut me open, turned me inside out, and run up and down my body with lodestone in search of a stray rebel ball. When they had me nearly killed, they would leave off a little while; but as soon as they saw signs of coming to life they went at it

again.   It 's a kind of gymnastics that a man can't
get fat on, try his best."

"I should think not"; and Kathie could n't help
laughing.

"But it 's through now. I feel like saying, with
Joe Gargery, 'And now, Pip, old chap,' (Pip, in this
instance, standing for country) 'we 've done our duty
by one another.' School is out, and Uncle Sam is
sending us home as fast as possible. I 've nothing to
do now but to be gloriously lazy, and have every one
wait upon me."

"O, I am so glad, so thankful," and Kathie pressed
the thin hands in her own, so soft and warm, "to
have you back here, when we were afraid — "

"It has been a hard struggle, little Kathie. I
shall never see a blue coat again without thinking
of what many a brave fellow has had to suffer. I
seem to have been feasted upon roses ; but hundreds
of them had no such luck."

"And to come to peace at last, — to know there
will be no more calls!"

"It certainly is good tidings of great joy. And
though I could n't be in at the last, losing all the
triumph and glory, I feel that I did a little good
work, and shall never regret the rest."

Her soft eyes answered him.

" And there is something else. I want to tell you that your precious words bore good fruit after many days. My dear child," drawing her closer to him until the silken curls swept his cheek, " I owe you more than I can ever express, ever pay. It was your sweet, simple daily life, and your unconscious heroism that first led me to think. I have heard hundreds of sermons, and had hosts of religious friends, but nothing ever touched me like your gentle firmness that night so long ago at my brother's, and your rare modesty afterward, and all your straightforward course, even when it involved pain and sacrifice. I can't exactly tell you how the truth and the peace came to me, enabling me to do my duty to God and man ; but when I was ill and helpless, and hovering on the verge of death, I want you to know that *His* love was infinitely precious to me. It took away all perplexity, all care and trouble, and gave me rest in the dreariest of nights. And as He suffered for us, so ought we to be willing to suffer for one another. I never realized before what a great and grand thing life was when obedience to God crowns it first of all. And even out there it seemed as if I was always taking lessons of you, remembering what you had said and done."

"O no, no!" she cried, with her utmost sweet humility. "I am not worthy of so much."

"My darling friend, I think you are one of God's own messengers. Through you I have found him, come to see him as he is, a tender, loving Father."

She hardly dared to taste the rich ripe fruit gathered here to her hand. It was such a sacred work to have guided another soul ever so little, and she could scarcely believe that it had come through her.

"Are you going to keep Kathie all the afternoon?" asked a soft, pleading voice.

Both started. For many minutes they had been silently thinking of the little steps that reached to God, made so much more simple and easy by the tender spirit-leading than all the learned philosophy of the world.

"O Miss Jessie!"

"Mrs. Meredith, if you please," he exclaimed with a little laugh in his tone. "There, you have kissed enough. Come, sit down and look at me. I am afraid you will forget about my being one of our country's noble sons."

Jessie might have been a little thinner with all her anxiety and watching, but she was the same dear, sweet friend, and Kathie thought prettier than ever, with her half shy, tender grace.

"He has grown very exacting," the young wife said, with a smile.

Kathie blushed. "It seems so odd for you to — be —"

"Married," exclaimed Mr. Meredith. "Why, what else could I do? When I was a poor, helpless log, unable to stir hand or foot, some one had to take pity upon me. She was very good, I assure you."

"As if I had not known it long before!" and a host of old memories rushed over Kathie.

"Is n't it odd," Mr. Meredith said, in a lower tone, taking his wife's hand, "that it was through Kathie we came to know each other? I can just see the picture she made in the great hall of the hotel, like a little wild-flower blown astray by a gust of wind."

Jessie thought of something else, — how she and Charlie were sitting by the cheerful fire one winter night, when he had expressed a desire to make her happy in some way, because she was always studying the pleasure of others. But for that she might never have known the Alstons so intimately, and of course —

There she had to stop with a dainty blush.

It was very odd, Kathie decided, in her simple child's way.

"And we have to thank Kathie for a good deal of delicacy in keeping our secret," Mr. Meredith said. "Circumstances gave it into her hands long ago."

She smiled a little. "What did Ada say?" she asked, rather shyly.

"I have not been favored with Ada's opinion, but she and her mother are to pay me a short visit presently. George wanted me to come immediately to New York, but I fancied Jessie must be a trifle homesick; and, to confess the truth, I was longing for a glimpse of Brookside. Have you begun gardening yet, Kathie? And tell me the story of the whole winter. I 'm just famishing for gossip."

Uncle Robert proposed returning presently, but they would not listen to his taking Kathie. Mr. Meredith begged her and Jessie to have tea up in the room, where he could look at them. His side was still very weak, and his journey had fatigued him too much to admit of his sitting up. "But I shall soon be about with a crutch," he announced, gayly.

Passing the lodge cottage again that evening, Kathie gave a tender thought to its inmates, and the childish longing for fairy power came back to her. No wand, nothing but a Fortunatus's purse with one piece of gold in it, and that could not do everything.

Kathie was up betimes the next morning. There were lessons to study, an exercise to write, and a music practice to be sandwiched in somewhere, for Mr. Lawrence was to come that afternoon. And her head was still so full of Mr. Meredith and dear Jessie.

"It will not do," she said, presently, to herself, when she found that she was listening to every bird, and watching the cloud of motes in the sunshine; so with that she set to work in good earnest.

Belle Hadden was loftier than ever on this day, and seemed to hold herself quite apart. "A new kink of grandeur," Emma Lauriston said.

Lottie Thorne always had the earliest news. Now she made sundry mysterious confidences, prefaced with, "Would you have believed it?"

"What is that, Lottie?" asked one of the girls.

"O, have n't you heard?" the face aglow with a sense of importance. "Papa told us last night, though I suppose it is all over. Poor Belle! Why, it would kill me!"

"But what *is* it?"

"About Mr. Hadden. He has been embezzling, or making false returns, or something, and charged the government with a great deal more than he supplied. Why, I believe it is almost a million! And he is in prison!"

"Not so bad as that," subjoined Sue Coleman, quietly.

"But he *is* in prison."

"Yes, there is some trouble, but maybe it will not amount to much."

"I should think she would be ashamed to show her face!"

"How can *she* help it?" said the softest and sweetest of voices. "It is very hard to punish her or make her answerable for her father's faults."

"What should you do, Kathie Alston, if you had been intimate with her?" It was Sue Coleman who spoke, and there was a husky strand in her voice.

"I should keep on just the same. It will be very painful for her to bear anyhow. Suppose it was one of us!"

"You don't know what hateful things she said about your uncle ever so long ago," pursued Lottie.

"But if they were false, her merely saying them could not make them true, you know."

It was a bit of philosophy quite new to the girls, though each one might have thought of it long before, and was one of the things that had been a great comfort to Kathie many a time.

"But this *is* true."

"It will be bitter enough to bear, then, without our adding to the burden"; and a tremulous color flitted over Kathie's fair face, not so much at what she had been saying as the fact that these girls were grouped around listening for her verdict.

"I don't believe she will come to-morrow," two or three voices decided.

They never knew how hard her coming was, how she had begged and entreated her mother to let her stay at home, and finally threatened *not* to go, when Mrs. Hadden had taken her in the carriage. There was no pride in her soul as she stepped out of it, only a bitter, haughty hatred.

"Don't act like a fool!" was her mother's parting advice. "The matter will soon blow over."

For Mrs. Hadden felt that she should not be utterly crushed. The deed of the house was in her name, and the furniture bills had been made out in the same manner, consequently that much was secure. Mr. Hadden had probably not done more than hundreds of others, and she felt confident that he would get out of it somehow. They had plenty of money, and could start afresh in a new place, but the people here should see that she was able to hold her head as high as the best of them.

There was a little bouquet on Belle's desk. No one knew who put it there. They would have suspected Kathie Alston, of course, if they had not seen her come in empty-handed, but no one guessed it was her second coming that morning.

The Brookside Standard copied the report, stating also that Mr. Hadden had asked a suspension of public opinion for the present.

"Do you suppose it is really true?" inquired Kathie of Uncle Robert.

"I believe Mr. Hadden's reputation does not stand very high, at the best. I can forgive a man who is tempted to retrieve himself by some desperate step, when on the brink of ruin; but the men who wronged our poor brave boys with clothing that was but half made, and food of the poorest kind, enriching themselves while the country was at her sorest need, do deserve punishment. Still, it would be hardly kind to begin by meting it out to his children."

"How terrible it must be, Uncle Robert, to know that some one you held dear was guilty of such a crime!"

"Yes, I think it would be worse than taking up poor and uncultivated people"; and a peculiar smile crossed his face. "You will have an opportunity to show your blue blood, Kathie. I believe I never knew a Conover who struck a fallen foe."

"Yes," she answered, wondering if it would be foolish to tell him about the flowers; but just then Freddy ran in, full of tribulation as usual.

Mr. Meredith improved rapidly. Kathie had to take him in her way some time during the day, or there was a most heart-rending complaint.

"It is so delightful to have them all love him so well!" she said to Aunt Ruth. "Charlie has a hero of his own now."

They received a long and characteristic letter from Rob, who wished he was a bombshell and could be dropped down into Brookside. The war was actually ended, and "Johnny was marching home," and everything had happened about right. "Only I am awful sorry about Mr. Morrison. I can't seem to believe but that he will come to light somewhere yet. It gave me such a strange feeling, — thinking, for a moment, if it *had* been Uncle Robert. We will try all our lives to make it up to Ethel. I will never tease her again, at any rate." Which was all the resolve in Rob's power at present.

CHAPTER XIII.

GOOD NEWS.

IT seemed to Kathie in these days as if she had her hands very full. The weeks were hardly long enough. Yet what could be left out? The daily call at the Darrells', or the Morrisons', for now Ethel looked to see her every day, and used to confide to her the sums that bothered, the thoughts that puzzled, and the many things which come to trouble little girls; and if sometimes Kathie considered them tiresome or foolish, she remembered how patient dear Aunt Ruth used to be with her in the old times, — and now she had Uncle Robert saved to her by Ethel's loss.

No, neither of those could be given up, nor the school-lessons, nor the music, nor even Sarah, who *was* improving.

The blue ribbon had delighted her exceedingly. Kathie said, very gently indeed, — that is, prefacing and ending it with something pleasant, — "I think it will be much prettier for your hair than any other color." That started Sarah upon a new tack.

"I wish you would tell me something about colors," she begged in her next letter. "I always remember how lovely you looked that night at the Fair, and some of the ladies too. I can't be pretty, I know, but I'd like to look nice, so that people would n't laugh at me. Now that I have begun, there are so many things that I want to know. Cousin Ellen helps me a good deal, and she is such a rest to mother. She has the pleasantest way of managing the children, and does such a deal of sewing. Father said I might raise all the chickens I wanted to this summer, and I think I'll buy a nice rocking-chair for the parlor. O, I have crocheted two beautiful tidies, and one of them is about as good as sold for two dollars and a half. If it is n't too much trouble, I would like to send the money to you, and let you buy me some books. You know what is pretty and interesting. And if you would only tell me what would be nice for summer dresses and a hat."

The ice being once broken, discussions upon dress followed quite frequently. When Kathie was in any doubt she referred the subject to Aunt Ruth. It was plain that Sarah was emerging from her crude and barbaric state, yet she showed no disposition thus far **to drift** over into the frothy **waves of** vanity. **With** her other knowledge seemed to come shrewd, practical self-knowledge.

Jim too had been made the happy recipient of some useful books. He seemed to have a great taste for wood-working, — "conjuring," his father said, — and talked a little of going to the city to learn a trade, but Mr. Strong had no fancy for giving him up now, when he was such a help.

"The farm is plenty large enough for **two**," Mr. Strong said, "and there 's no life so independent."

But Mr. Conover felt that it ought to be rendered interesting as well. So he asked Jim to come down to Cedarwood and take a look around, which delighted the youth greatly, and gave him some new ideas.

The rumors concerning Belle Hadden's father proved too true. It was an aggravated case, and each day brought new circumstances to light. It was useless to think of holding their position in Brookside. Acquaintances began to make ceremonious calls, or bow coldly. A few of the girls in school openly rejoiced.

"Thank the Lord my father never stole nor cheated," said Mary Carson. "I 'd rather be a plebeian than a thief."

15

The mortification was too much. Belle begged and prayed that she might be allowed to leave Brookside, and finally a visit to an aunt was determined upon. She was a queen to the last moment, though, and said her good-bys to the few with a haughty grace.

"Thus endeth the reign of the patricians," commented Emma Lauriston.

There was a grave, perplexed light in Sue Coleman's eyes.

"Belle was real fascinating," she said; "but I wonder that we — that some of us had n't more sense last winter. We all went to persecuting and ruling out Kathie Alston, who bore it all like a saint. Belle had courage and pride, but there was something nobler in Kathie." Yet Sue knit her brows in silent perplexity.

"But there is another view of it that puzzles me, after all," she said, breaking her long silence. "Where *do* people make a distinction? Now suppose Kathie Alston invited this *protégée* of hers to her house, and you or I should drop in — it would look ill-bred to take Kathie away from her guest, and yet it is not likely her talk would interest us much. Then as Kathie grows larger — well, it is all of a muddle in my brain. I dare say these Strongs are good, honest, respectable people, and—there is no use in smoothing it over—Mr. Hadden was dreadfully dishonest. All their grandeur and fine clothes belong by right to some one else. And yet they are allowed to go into the best society. Is it *quite* right?"

"Not the *very* best, perhaps," returned Emma, slowly. "A good many people do insist upon worth, virtue, honesty, and all that."

"And then, as Kathie said, Belle was not to blame for her father's sins."

"It seems to me now that Belle's mistake was in trying to decide who should be greatest, and pushing down all who did not exactly suit her. She had no right to be the judge."

"Who of us has? And here is another question. You remember Mrs. Duncan? She went to the city about a fortnight ago, and had a business offer. First, I must tell you that she was very elegantly brought up, but her father died, and somehow the fortune melted into thin air. She went to visit an aunt, and met Mr. Duncan, who was cashier in a bank. They have always lived very nicely,—stylishly, Belle would say,—but now they have nothing, and Mrs. Duncan has no friends who can take care of her. She has forgotten a good deal of her French and her other accomplishments, and teachers' situations are hard to get. Well, a Mrs. Marsh in the city has offered Mrs. Duncan eight hundred dollars a year to take a position in her millinery establishment. She has a marvellous faculty for trimming, — equal to any French woman. And why would n't she be just as good and just as much of a lady if she did take it? Will it make her coarse and vulgar?"

"No," answered Emma, decisively.

"Yet I dare say the Hadden children would not be allowed to associate with the Duncan girls. I cannot seem to get at the wrong, nor where it comes in."

"I believe, after all, Kathie Alston has the secret, — the little leaven which leavens the whole lump."

"Only some of us object to being leavened"; and Sue finished with a laugh.

But though Kathie had not heard the talk, there was a secret uneasiness in her soul as well. Sarah Strong was begging her to come up to Middleville again, and Uncle Robert believed the relaxation would do her good.

"Mamma," she said, thoughtfully, "there are one or two puzzles that I cannot make quite clear to my own mind."

"What is the matter now? Any new gift for Sarah?"

"Not a gift exactly, but — a great pleasure. When I was with them in the wagon that day, and they were both so cordial and warm-hearted, it appeared rude, or at least impolite, not to ask them to call here. Mrs. Strong said, 'Sarah would n't look well among your grand people'; but there was such a sad, wistful look in Sarah's eyes, as if somehow she felt that she was shut out."

"And you would like to have her come?" returned Mrs. Alston, with a smile.

"I was thinking how happy it would make her, mamma. I don't believe she ever saw so many pretty things together in her life, — and she is so fond of them."

"And what puzzles you?"

"Whether it would be quite — I don't mean that I am too proud," catching herself with a quick breath, while a scarlet flush quivered from brow to chin.

"Whether it would be proper, — is that what you mean?" asked her mother.

"Yes"; and Kathie began to twist the fringe of the nearest tidy.

"Miss Jessie asked you to her house, you know. We lived very plainly then, and you had to wear a cheap delaine for best dress all winter."

"Then you think I may?" she exclaimed, joyously, while her soft eyes brightened.

"It all depends upon the manner of the asking. I think she might come some Saturday when you were alone and have a very pleasant visit. It is not likely she would enjoy meeting several of the girls here."

"O mamma, I should ask no one!"

"Not because we should be so ashamed of Sarah, but on account of her feelings. It is best for little girls to exercise tact, as well as grown-up people; and sometimes it proves awkward work trying to make different kinds or sets harmonize. By observing a few simple rules, and studying the comfort of both parties, you may be able to give all greater happiness."

"Then, when I go up, I shall invite Sarah in so cordial a manner that her mother will see that I mean every word."

" Yes; for the unkindest invitation of all is to ask people purely out of compliment."

The smooth brow was slightly shadowed again. " Mamma," she said, in a low tone, " can people — grown-up ladies, I mean — get along without saying or doing things that they really do not mean to have taken in earnest ? "

" They had better not say them. A Christian woman will be truthful first of all; but it is not necessary to make candor a cloak for the indulgence of unkind or heartless remarks. Religion, it seems to me, holds the essence of true politeness, — to do unto others as you would have them do unto you."

The next day Kathie was quite late in getting home, having stopped at the Darrells'. Uncle Robert and mamma were up in Aunt Ruth's room.

" What will you give me for a letter with a grand seal as if it came from the very Commander-in-Chief or the President ? Look! To ' Miss Kathie Alston.' What correspondent have you in Washington, we would all like to know ? "

Uncle Robert held the letter above her head. A bold, peculiar handwriting that she had never seen before. Whose could it be ?

"I am sure I don't know," coloring with interest and excitement. "I have a gold piece in my purse."

"I will not be quite so mercenary as that. You shall tell us whom it is from."

Kathie took the letter and broke it open so as not to destroy the seal, saw the beginning, — "My dear little friend," — ran her eye over the two pages without taking in anything, and looked at the signature.

"O," with a cry of surprise, "it is from General Mackenzie! Why," — and then she began to read in good earnest, — "Mr. Morrison is alive, safe! General Mackenzie found him. O Uncle Robert!"

She could not finish the rest, but buried her head on Uncle Robert's shoulder to have a good little cry out of pure joy and thankfulness.

"Shall I read it aloud?"

She placed the letter in his hand.

"My dear little Friend, — I dare say you will be surprised at receiving a letter from a busy old soldier like me, but I met with an incident a few days ago with which you are so intimately connected that I cannot resist the good excuse. Of course all the glorious news and rejoicing has reached you, but we here on the spot are hearing new things daily, some joyful, but many sad. We went up the James River one morning to a small settlement originally negro quarters, where we heard a number of wounded prisoners had been taken. We found thirty poor fellows in all, who had suffered terribly from neglect, for though the negroes were well-meaning and very warm-hearted, they were miserably poor and ignorant. Half a dozen of the soldiers had been very ill from fevers, and upon questioning them I found one was — whom do you think? — your uncle's substitute, a William Morrison. That took me back to last winter at once, and to my little friend, so do not wonder if we had a good long talk about you and the beautiful Cedarwood of which I have heard so much. I believe it did the poor fellow a world of good. He was wounded and taken prisoner, and brought up here by the negroes, as far as I can learn. In those few days of our final successes the small events were overlooked in the glory of the grander ones. His wound was not very severe, but fever set in, and for three weeks he was delirious. About ten days ago he wrote home, but he was not sure that his messenger was reliable. He was much better, and we despatched those who could travel to head-quarters at once. I fancy that he will be mustered out as soon as possible. If his friends should not have heard, will you please inform them ? He holds you all in such warm and grateful remembrance that it was delightful to talk to him. I rejoice with you that he is safe, and I do not question but that he has done a soldier's whole duty. I thought I discerned in him the spirit of another little soldier, who I dare say finds some battles to fight. Give my regards to your family, and do not feel surprised when I tell you that you may expect me at Cedarwood some day before long.

"Truly yours,
"W. MACKENZIE, U. S. A."

"It hardly seems possible !" Kathie said, with a sob. "But they have not heard, and they will be so glad !"

Uncle Robert began to pace the room, much moved. Of late death had appeared such a certainty, and though he knew the life had been freely given for his, his first emotions were those of devout gratitude to God that this sacrifice had not been required.

Then he paused before Kathie. "My little darling," he said, "it is *your* good news. And though the Morrisons may hear it in a day or two from other sources, we owe it to them immediately. Will you go?"

Kathie wanted to very much, but O, how was she ever to get through with it! Her voice seemed to be all a quiver of tears.

"Would you like me to accompany you?

"If you will."

So Kathie bathed her face and tried to rub the little throbs out of her temples. In a few moments she was ready, and the two walked down the avenue.

"There *cannot* be any mistake?" she exclaimed, pausing at the door.

"O no."

Grandmother was holding the baby, who had a slight cold and fever. Ethel sat at the window, hemming some breadths of ruffling. She sprang up and brought out chairs for them, and after one or two little inquiries went back to her work. Oddly enough the conversation ceased for a few moments, and in the silence Kathie fancied that she heard her heart beat, it was in such a tumult.

"I believe Kathie has some news for you," announced Mr. Conover, gravely.

Kathie rose and twined her arms around Ethel's neck.

"It is this," she said, all in a tremble, — "I cannot tell it as I ought, but your dear father is alive, Ethel, and is coming home soon."

"Not William! Miss Kathie!" and grandmother almost let the baby fall.

"Yes," replied Mr. Conover; "we heard to-day. I have brought the letter."

"The Lord be praised!" Then grandmother came over to Kathie, but she and Ethel were crying softly in each other's arms.

"Child, are you one of God's own — Heaven-sent? for you bring us joy continually."

"But it was sent to me," Kathie said, over a great break and falter. "If I could have made it so in the beginning, — but I could n't, and God kept him safely. We all waited and prayed."

"And I despaired! I am worse than doubting Thomas! Ah, how good God is to us all!"

Mrs. Morrison entered with a pail of milk "O," she exclaimed, "you have had news! Have they found his body?"

"His body and soul. He will be back shortly. The tidings came through a friend of Kathie."

"Dear Ethel, little one, it is blessed news! You would never have wanted for love and kindness while Hugh and I were alive; but there's no love quite like a parent's. How Hugh will rejoice! He never could give him up altogether."

"Mr. Conover has a letter to read," said grandmother.

Little did General Mackenzie imagine that his words would bring so great a joy. They all listened breathlessly, and then wanted it read over again to lengthen out the good news. And when at dusk Uncle Robert declared they must go, they all begged for Kathie to stay and drink tea, and would take no refusal.

"But I must return," said Uncle Robert, "or the table will be kept for us both."

Mrs. Morrison made some biscuits, and brought out her china, as well as a damask table-cloth. Hugh, coming in, wondered at the feast; but Ethel's first word told him all. She, poor child, was brimful of joy. It did one good to look at the roses on her cheeks, and hear the little laughs that came for joy, and yet were so near to tears.

When Kathie reached home she was absolutely tired with all the excitement, and mamma said there must be no lessons that night; so they took the lounge in the shaded half-light of the library, and Kathie laid her head in Uncle Robert's lap, for it almost ached. And there they had a tender talk.

"But we shall never forget it," she said. "It seems as if it would help me to remember all the pains and sorrows and burdens that we can try to bear for one another."

"It is what God means us to learn and to do. 'For no man liveth unto himself, and no man dieth unto himself.'"

"And we are all so oddly linked in with one another, — such a little thing brought the Morrisons here, and then my meeting General Mackenzie gave him an interest. The news would have come in a day or two, I suppose; but, Uncle Robert, it seemed so good, since he risked his life in your place, that we should be the first to take the joyful tidings to them. I have n't anything in the world to ask."

"Yes, my darling, I am so glad that General Mackenzie did find him; and more than glad that our brave soldiers can return to their own pleasant fire-sides."

"Neither of *our* soldiers was very grand in the world's estimation, that is, as to position, but they have both suffered a good deal for the cause. It is so sweet to think that, though the world knows nothing about it, God remembers."

"And that no act of self-denial or heroism goes without its reward there. It is hard sometimes to see it passed so unnoticed in this world, but I suppose that is where patience needs to have her perfect work."

Kathie wrote a little note to Rob the next morning, beside getting her lessons; and before the day ended they had a letter from Mr. Morrison himself, announcing that he was to be sent home on a furlough.

"I shall have a dangerous rival," exclaimed Mr. Meredith, in his teasing tone,; "and when General Mackenzie comes I expect to be quite overshadowed. No stars nor bars nor shoulder-straps, — nothing but a poor unknown private! What good could he do?"

"He followed his captain and did his duty."

"Good!" exclaimed Charlie, who was standing beside his brother-in-law. "You will never find Kathie being caught by the glitter and show."

The old smile twinkled in Mr. Meredith's eyes.

"Well, I will promise not to be *very* jealous. Only you know you sent me off to war, so you ought to allow me some special indulgence."

"I!" exclaimed Kathie, coloring violently.

"Yes, you cannot disown me; I am one of your soldiers. Dear little Kathie, I hope always to be true to my colors."

The last was uttered in a low tone, but it brought a more vivid flush than the preceding sentence. Though now her eyes were downcast, yet in her heart of hearts she understood.

"It seems as if Rob ought to come home in the general returning. How glad I shall be to see the dear old fellow!"

Was Rob fighting the good fight?

CHAPTER XIV.

PUT TO THE TEST.

THE days were so long and pleasant now that Uncle Robert thought they would not start for Middleville until after dinner, especially as there would be a bright moon in the evening. Kathie had written a little note to Sarah, and now the two started in high satisfaction. For since the good news about Mr. Morrison Kathie seemed full of happiness and content.

The place looked less dreary than in winter, though the houses appeared rather more shabby by contrast. One or two were being painted, which would shame the rest sadly. But the hillsides were taking on an emerald tint, and groups of cows were wandering about as if patiently waiting for the grass to grow into nibbling length.

Sarah was standing by the gate, watching for them. A very decided change *had* come over her. She was taller and looked less stout, her complexion was not

16

so rough and red, her dress, a striped green and white gingham, fitted nicely, and was finished at the throat by a linen collar. She had eschewed waterfalls and rolls, though she laughingly admitted to Kathie afterwards that it was because she could n't get her hair up to look like anything. But the great thick coil was really beautiful, and the green ribbon very becoming.

She had changed somewhat in manners as well, being less boisterous and effusive. Indeed, Kathie thought her very lady-like as she ushered them into the house.

"Is your brother anywhere about?" asked Uncle Robert. "If so, I will go and find him while you girls have a talk."

"He is up in the lot. Steve will show you, or, better yet, call him."

Then she led Kathie into the parlor. There were green paper shades at the windows, which softened the light in the room, and Kathie's first glance took in a world of improvements.

Sarah colored with a little conscious pride as she led her to a veritable modern sofa, instead of the old stiff one, worn at the edges.

"Take off your hat and sack," she said, with a touch of bashfulness.

Kathie complied.

"I am so glad to see you. I have such a host of things to tell you."

"And you have been out gathering violets. How pretty and spring-like they are !"

"Yes, Jim helped me. We thought you would like them so much. And I have been trying to — to get fixed up a little. It cannot be anything like your house, but somehow I want it as nice as I can make it. Jim is so good too, and Cousin Nelly; and I am so happy sometimes that I really wonder if I be I, like the old woman."

"I am very glad"; and Kathie gave the hand a squeeze in her own tender little fashion.

"I want to tell you all before any one comes in. Isn't it delightful to have this sofa? I made father half a dozen shirts all by myself, and he was so pleased, — you can hardly think! He gave me twelve dollars to spend just as I pleased; but I told mother I would rather let it go towards a new sofa than to buy the finest dress. Nelly said it would be so much more comfortable than that hard, shabby thing, that looked as if it might have come out of Noah's Ark. So mother gave me fifteen, — she has all the money for the milk and butter and eggs, — and when father heard of it he added three more. I was afraid he would think I wanted to be too fine, but he only laughed a little. Mother and Nelly went to the city and bought it. I was so glad that I could have cried for joy, and I know father is very proud of it, though he does not say it in so many words."

"It is a very nice one, and furnishes the room quite prettily, beside the comfort of it."

"Jim made me this table, and Cousin Nelly and I covered it with paper and then varnished it over, and we have a pretty chintz one up stairs. Nelly and I have a room together now. I can keep every-thing so much more tidy than when the children pulled all the rubbish about. And look at my two new pictures!"

They were large colored engravings, — one, "The Wood-Gatherers," and the other the interior of a German peasant's cottage, where the mother was putting a babe to sleep in its odd wicker cradle.

"Jim bought them at a newspaper-stand one day,

and only paid twelve cents apiece for them. He's powerful — no, I mean very fond of them. I am trying to leave off all those old-fashioned words and expressions. Then he made the frames, and Nelly and I covered them with pine-cones."

They certainly were very creditable.

"But how industrious you must be!" exclaimed Kathie. "You still go to school?"

"Yes. I would n't give that up for half the world. You see Cousin Nelly helps mother a good deal, and she helps me too. I have been telling her ever so much about you, how good and lovely you were. But O, was n't I a clown and an ignoramus when you first saw me! I don't wonder that girl laughed, though it was hateful in her; but I shall never, never forget how kind you were. O Miss Kathie, it seems to me if the real nice people in the world *would* only help the others a bit, we should get along so much faster. I feel as if I 'd had it in me all the time, — a great hungry longing for something, — and I find now that it is beauty and order and knowledge."

Sarah's face was in a glow, and her steady, ardent eyes held in them a soft and tender light. It seemed to Kathie that she was really pretty, or something more than that, — electrified with soul beauty.

"Father pretends that he is afraid I shall get too proud and not be good for anything, though he was ever so much pleased when he saw the parlor in such nice order. And he thought the shirts a wonder. I shall not be sixteen until November, and there are girls older than I who could not do it. In vacation I am going to make Jim a whole new set of nice ones with linen bosoms."

It seemed to Kathie that there was very little danger of Sarah's being spoiled by acquiring knowledge.

"You deserve the utmost credit," she returned, in her simple manner, that had in it no shade of patronage or condescension.

"I ought to do something for the pains and trouble you have taken."

"It is a pleasure too."

"Miss Kathie, you are so different from some rich people. I wonder what makes it?"

A soft color stole up into her face. She would fain have kept silence, but she saw that Sarah was waiting for an answer. "I think it is because mamma and Uncle Robert believe that wealth was not

given for purely personal or selfish purposes. It is
God's treasure, and we are to put it out at usury, like
the parable of the talents, and the usury means making other people happy if we can."

"Then I suppose I ought to try and make some
one happy?"

"Do you not?" asked Kathie, simply.

"Yes, I do occasionally when it is quite a trouble.
The children beg me to read to them, — they are
so fond of stories; and now father always wants me
to read our paper to him. It comes on Saturday and
he is always so tired that night. Still, that is n't —"
and Sarah paused as if she despaired of rendering her
meaning clear to her young listener.

"I think Uncle Robert would say that *is* it surely.
Once in a while we can do larger things; but is n't
it the little deeds that require the most patience? It
is the steps that make up the whole path."

"So it is. I never thought of it before"; and she
smiled, relieved. "You believe, Miss Kathie, that
what we do at home is just as good in God's eyes as
if we did it for a stranger? It almost seemed to me
as if I ought to go out and look for some poor ignorant person instead."

"Both are doing good in different ways. Maybe it is best to learn to do the good at home first"; and Kathie remembered her early efforts in assisting her mother.

"I want father to see that all my knowledge and my queer likes, as he calls them, will not really spoil me. Grandmother Strong has just such old-fashioned notions. She thinks my going to school perfectly absurd. But Cousin Ellen says the world has changed a good deal since grandmother was young."

"And I have brought your books," said Kathie, when there was a pause of sufficient length. "The three are half of a pretty set; some time you may like to get the others."

"You are so kind. I hated to bother you, but I knew you could make the best choice."

"It was no trouble at all, — Uncle Robert did it, and he bought them for half a dollar less than their usual price."

"I am so much obliged!" and Sarah's face was in a grateful glow.

Kathie had wanted very much to supply the other three.

"If Sarah were poor," replied Uncle Robert, "I

should not object; but when such a person asks you to do a favor, it is best to keep simply to the letter of the request. If you gave her so much more, she would hesitate about asking you to do such a thing a second time, that is, if she possessed any real delicacy."

Kathie saw the force of the reasoning.

Presently Cousin Ellen came down. She was a neat, commonplace-looking woman of about thirty, but with a good deal of shrewd sense in her dark gray eyes. Her black calico dress was the perfection of tidiness, and the merest little ruff of book-muslin edged it round the neck.

Kathie liked her very much. She had been in the midst of the war operations for the last three years, and to please Sarah she related numberless incidents that interested Kathie exceedingly. Then she had to go up stairs and see their room, take a tour around, and have all the flower-beds explained to her, to go to the barn and inspect several new articles Jim was making. Uncle Robert and the boys joined them here, and Kathie was introduced to Mr. Strong.

"Don't you have a little too much in-doors and study?" he asked, pleasantly. "I should n't like to see one of my gals look as white as you do."

"O, she is always white, father," said Sarah, admiringly.

"And she has plenty of roses too, for the most part," explained Uncle Robert, "only for the last few weeks she has been rather overtaxed, I think. We have had a returned soldier, a very dear friend, ill, and been in great anxiety about another."

"Thank the Lord for all who 've come home safe," said Mr. Strong, in his clear, forcible tone, and every one of them felt like adding an "Amen" to it.

Martha ran out to call them to tea.

There was the great table spread, and all the children around it, even to fatherless Willie, who would never need a friend while Jotham Strong lived.

It was a very enjoyable supper. The new influence was perceptible even in sturdy Mrs. Strong, who took a little pains that she might not shame Sarah before her company.

Kathie asked Mrs. Strong to let Sarah come down some Saturday and make her a visit.

"I can't exactly explain, Miss Kathie, and I hate to be ungrateful for your kindness, but I feel as if you and your friends were above Sarah. Folks ain't all alike, and I s'pose the Lord did n't mean 'em to

be, but I don't want Sarah laughed at, and I don't
want any one to think she's trying to crowd in
We're plain, old-fashioned people"—

Mrs. Strong paused, very red in the face.

"No one will think that at Cedarwood," answered
Kathie, softly.

So presently the promise was given. In a fortnight Cousin Ellen and Sarah were to go down to
Brookside to do some shopping. Ellen wanted to
call on several of the relatives, but Sarah might go
at once to Cedarwood.

"I expect it will be like a little bit of heaven," the
girl whispered. "I never was in a real elegant house
in all my life."

Kathie described her visit to Aunt Ruth in glowing terms. "I think it *is* delightful to be rich, after
all," she said, contentedly. "You can make so many
people happy."

"And while you study the happiness of others and
your duty towards them the riches will hardly prove
a snare," returned Aunt Ruth.

Before another week had ended they had a new
joy for which to be very thankful, — the return of
Mr. Morrison. He still looked a little pale and thin,

but had improved wonderfully since the day when
General Mackenzie found him in the forlorn negro
quarters. Glad enough he was to get home to his
little Ethel, who hardly let him go out of her sight.
Nothing would do but that the whole family must
come down to the cottage and drink tea.

"I must express my obligations once more to
you," said Uncle Robert, in the evening; "and I
am most grateful to God for your return, and that
he did not require so costly a sacrifice at my hands."

"He knows that I am glad enough to come back;
but if you 'll believe me, sir, it was a great comfort,
when I thought myself dying, that it was in your
stead, and that your life, so much more valuable than
mine, had been spared. I believe you would have
sorrowed for me truly, — and Miss Kathie here, —
as well as my own."

Kathie took his hand. "I 've been thinking of
this ever since the night you offered to go: 'Greater
love hath no man than this, that a man lay down his
life for his friends.' "

The sweet voice trembled a little. It would always have a tender strand in it when it came to that
verse.

"Ah, Miss Kathie, those precious words were for the Saviour of us all. What can we ever do to merit them?" and the soldier drew the back of his hand across his eyes.

"God gives the grace to weak human nature," Uncle Robert said, with solemn sweetness.

Walking home, Kathie started from her revery. "Now if Rob could only come back," she exclaimed, "our soldiers would all be together. You remember the day he was so elated about the draft?"

"Yes. Dear Rob! I hope he has done good service. I am very anxious to see him again."

Then Kathie began to count on the promised visit. "It is not because I am so proud of Cedarwood, or the handsome things in it," she explained to Uncle Robert, "though I do think them all very lovely; but it will be such a pleasure to her, — just as my going to Miss Jessie's when we were so poor."

"I understand"; and he smiled.

There had been quite a discussion about having a second girl. Uncle Robert fancied that Kathie's further knowledge of household details had better be postponed until she had less upon her hands. Jane Maybin, who had been a good deal out of health lately, and unable to work in the factory, as the dust irritated her lungs and made her cough, was quite anxious to take the situation. What with company and increasing social duties, Mrs. Alston found her time much interrupted.

Hannah did all the sweeping on Friday, but it was a heavy tax ; so Kathie only dusted awhile on Saturday morning, cut fresh flowers and arranged them, and busied herself about little odds and ends. Mrs. Alston decided to have Jane, and Aunt Ruth took a walk over to the cottage.

Kathie waited in a peculiar state of anxiety. Lucy and Annie Gardiner had proposed to come over that very afternoon, but she preferred to have Sarah quite alone, that she might feel free to enjoy everything.

It was almost twelve when she reached Cedarwood. Kathie was haunting the cottage, where she could have a good look down the street, but she hardly recognized the figure at first. It seemed as if Sarah grew every week. She looked quite like a young lady, Kathie thought. Her light gray dress was trimmed with several rows of blue ribbon, and the sack, matching it, made a very neat suit. Her white straw hat was trimmed with blue, and a cluster of crisp, fresh flowers, that looked almost good enough to be natural. There was nothing in that outfit to be ashamed of.

"O," she exclaimed, with a long breath, "it 's like going into the Garden of Eden! The house and the trees, and that lovely lake! I should want to be out of doors forever."

"Uncle Robert has promised to row us around the lake this afternoon. A month later it will be much more beautiful. Did you finish your shopping?"

"O yes, though we were bothered a good deal, and that made me later. Nelly wanted me to go to dinner at Cousin Rachel's."

"I am glad that you did not."

Sarah could not be hurried into the house. She wanted to view the fountain, the groups of evergreens, the broad porch, and fancy just how the roses and honeysuckle would look. But presently they entered. Kathie led her up stairs to her room, to lay aside her hat.

"O, I don't wonder Jim said it was a palace!" she exclaimed, with breathless delight. "What a lovely room! Why, it 's pretty enough for any one's parlor!"

Kathie smiled a little, remembering the day on which she had thought it wonderful as well.

Sarah was hardly satisfied with her inspection when the bell rang for dinner. In the hall they met Aunt Ruth, and in the dining-room Kathie introduced Sarah to her mother.

A girl with less natural adaptation or ambition might have been very awkward. But Sarah had watched Kathie to some purpose, and now gave herself courage with the thought that she could not go far astray if she copied Kathie. To be sure she blushed and hesitated a little, and, as she afterward confessed at home, "trembled all over"; but she did acquit herself very creditably.

"I can scarcely realize that it is the same girl who wrote you the Christmas letter," whispered Mrs. Alston in a soft aside, and Kathie smiled gratefully at her mother's commendation.

Then the two girls began a regular tour about the house. The pictures, the statues, the furniture, Aunt Ruth's beautiful bay-window still full of vines and flowers, and the abundance of books, were so many marvels to Sarah. And here, in the midst of all this beauty, hung her lichen. The tears of delight came to her eyes, in spite of her strong effort at repression.

"Now if you would only play and sing for me," she pleaded, bashfully. "You 're so good that I hate to ask anything."

"With pleasure."

It seemed as if Sarah could never get enough music. She listened as if she was entranced, the new spiritual light coming into her eyes, showing the strong and earnest capabilities of her soul.

Uncle Robert looked in upon them.

"I think you had better go out on the lake now," he said. "The air is so delightfully soft."

Sarah sighed. "I cannot imagine which is the best, everything is such a pleasure."

"We will have some music when we return. You will like the sail, I know."

They found their hats and ran down the broad steps. Quite a party were coming up the drive. Charlie and Dick, Mr. and Mrs. Meredith, and O, joy! this tall, soldierly man could be no other than General Mackenzie!

"My dear, dear young friend"; and, stooping, he kissed the forehead in his grave, tender fashion.

17

"So you see I have surprised you this time,"
laughed Mr. Meredith. "Where were you going
gypsy fashion ?"

"To the lake, but it does n't matter." There was
no Uncle Robert to help her, so she turned to where
Sarah stood blushing and abashed, drew her kindly
forward, and gave her an introduction to each one.
Dick connected her with the party and Belle Hadden
at once.

"Kathie was right to stand up for her," was his
mental verdict. "There are plenty of worse-looking
and worse-behaved girls in the world."

At this junction Uncle Robert joined them. The
whole party entered the parlor. Kathie seated Sarah
by herself, and General Mackenzie joined them.
Mrs. Alston and Aunt Ruth were summoned, and the
conversation became most genial. And when Sarah
ventured a remark, frightened half to death the
moment afterward, General Mackenzie smiled and
answered her. Dick Grayson, anxious to see "what
kind of stuff she was made of," came round to the
back of the *tête-à-tête*, and joined the talk.

But the wonders had not all come to an end. The
door-bell sounded again, and Hannah ushered two

young ladies into the hall. Kathie caught a glimpse of the faces, — Sue Coleman and Emma Lauriston.

They saw Dick and Charlie and the grand soldier beside this plain-looking girl, — some of the Darrells, maybe, — and, accepting Kathie's cordial invitation, joined the group.

" Miss Strong," Kathie said, with sweet, gracious simplicity; and Sue for a moment was abashed. Something in Dick's face announced the truth.

General Mackenzie did not seem to think her beneath him. Just now she was speaking of her cousin's husband and their having Mrs. Gilbert and Willie at home.'

" Miss Strong," he said, gravely, " I honor your parents for the act. There will be so many widows and orphans for whom the scanty pension will be as nothing. But the generous-hearted men and women who open their houses to these poor unfortunates pay our dead soldiers a higher compliment, and evince a truer appreciation of their gallant heroism, than if they made grand processions and built marble monuments."

Sarah blushed with embarrassment, and some deep, delicate feeling that she could not have expressed.

She had not done it boastingly ; indeed, until this moment, she had hardly thought of any special kindliness in the deed.

Actually complimented by General Mackenzie ! Lottie Thorne would have died of envy.

Somehow the time ran away very fast. They went out on the lawn in the sunshine, when Sue and Emma discovered that they must go, and the two boys walked with them. Then it came Sarah's turn, as she had promised to be at Cousin Rachel's by five.

"I 've had such a lovely, lovely time, Miss Kathie, though I felt dreadfully frightened when your grand company came ; but they were all so — so nice that I quite forgot about being an awkward country girl. And is n't General Mackenzie plain and charming ? — yes, that is the very word. I don't believe General Grant is a bit nicer. I shall tell mother just what he said. It will help to make up for the girls laughing about her bonnet."

Kathie had a simple gift to send to Baby Lily. Then the girls said a lingering good-by to each other, and Kathie went back to her hero.

"I must take the night return train," he declared,

"on account of important business in Washington; but if you will allow me to visit you in the summer, and bring my son, I will accept it as a great favor."

Uncle Robert gave him a most cordial invitation.

"And, my little friend, I must congratulate you that your soldiers did their duty without flinching, even in the most trying moments. It is not our lives only, but our wills, our comforts and pleasures, that we are required to give up. And I am thankful that God watched over them every hour, and sent them back safely at last."

"I think they were braver than I, sometimes," Kathie answered, in a low tone. "After all, I have done so little; I do not deserve the praise." Her voice seemed to lose itself in a tender humility.

"My dear child, I know what you thought of the other warfare. It is a soldier's duty to bring in all the recruits that he can. God will clothe them in his righteousness, and make the path plain before them as they go to do battle with the arch-enemy. He only asks us to lead them to him. You are doing this in a brave, steady manner."

There were tears in Kathie's downcast eyes; but Mr. Meredith's hand stole over her shoulder, and their fingers met with a clasp that was more expressive than words.

"People often look too far off for duties," continued the old soldier. "We are to take up the task that lies before us, even if it does not seem to wear the grace of the heroic. God knows when and where to add the golden fruit. Some day, my little girl, we will have a long talk about these matters."

The soft spring-twilight was falling as they said good-by to General Mackenzie. The grave, kindly eyes rested last of all on the child's simple, earnest face.

Mr. and Mrs. Meredith went also when Uncle Robert drove the General to the station. Kathie sat by the window, peering out into the darkness, long after the sound of the wheels had ceased. One star came out presently.

Shining on and on. The old, old lesson, the child's purpose growing stronger with the passing years, and Kathie prayed that as her soldiers had been faithful, she also might be faithful unto the end.

Cambridge: Electrotyped and Printed by Welch, Bigelow, & Co.